MWUAJI

(Assassin)

Janoesha Harbour Book 5

M C Williams

BALBOA.PRESS
A DIVISION OF HAY HOUSE

Balboa Press books may be ordered through booksellers or by contacting:

Balboa Press
A Division of Hay House
1663 Liberty Drive
Bloomington, IN 47403
www.balboapress.com
844-682-1282

Because of the dynamic nature of the Internet, any web addresses or
links contained in this book may have changed since publication and
may no longer be valid. The views expressed in this work are solely those
of the author and do not necessarily reflect the views of the publisher,
and the publisher hereby disclaims any responsibility for them.

The author of this book does not dispense medical advice or prescribe the use
of any technique as a form of treatment for physical, emotional, or medical
problems without the advice of a physician, either directly or indirectly. The
intent of the author is only to offer information of a general nature to help
you in your quest for emotional and spiritual well-being. In the event you use
any of the information in this book for yourself, which is your constitutional
right, the author and the publisher assume no responsibility for your actions.

Any people depicted in stock imagery provided by Getty Images are
models, and such images are being used for illustrative purposes only.
Certain stock imagery © Getty Images.

Print information available on the last page.

Library of Congress Control Number: 2022913160
ISBN: 979-8-7652-3134-0 (sc)
ISBN: 979-8-7652-3133-3 (hc)
ISBN: 979-8-7652-3135-7 (e)

Balboa Press rev. date: 07/15/2022

CONTENTS

MAIN CHARACTERS

1. Moses Uatobuu (aka) Silverback
2. Walt Buyer
3. Jeff Acheampong
4. Sterling Myers
5. Oscar Acheampong
6. Steve Matherson
7. Stacey Lane
8. Len O'Donnell
9. Terrance Banes
10. Stanley Metcalf
11. Joe Anhime
12. Rich Kessler
13. Chris Haddon
14. Alvin Powers
15. Bailey Gcobani
16. Otis Bryne
17. Peach McFarlen
18. Carmen Ayala
19. Shawn Morris
20. Jillian Rous
21. Lionel Davis
22. Doug Fenwell
23. Gary Adcliff
24. James T Haddler
25. David Bankole
26. Dedra Bankole
27. Dennis Moore
28. Roy Overmill
29. Hanson Abioye
30. Dean Chamapiwa
31. Ken Powell
32. Colonel Martez Jimenez
33. Rochelle Haddler
34. Jackson Ames (aka) Matthew Perez
35. Ray Gatlain

March 1ˢᵗ 1992, Kano Nigeria

Kano, Nigeria is a city located in the north of the country, that is where thirty-one year old Oscar Acheampong and his wife live with their two sons, David who is ten and Jeffery who is seven. Oscar worked at the local university as a English Professor, he spent most of his time editing term-papers and thesis. Oscar got the job at the university when he was living in Bangassou a city in the Central African Republic, that is where him and his kids were born, his wife is from Tanzania but grew up in Bangassou. Oscar worked as a grade-school teacher in Bangassou, the school was owned by a wealthy African business-man who had a reputation in using the local militia as his security. This concerned Oscar but the job paid well and he had a family to support, it took him a year and a half to land a job at the university. When he got the job he was so happy, he now had the opportunity to move his family out of the military runned city of Bangassou, the only thing was he was cutting his contract at the grade-school short, he had eleven months left on his contract but he still decided to sign his release-papers. This didn't sit well with the owner of the school, he felt he would lose money with Oscar leaving and on top of that Oscar received a severance package, this enraged the owner, he felt Oscar stole from him. Oscar was so worried about his family's safety that he booked an overnight flight to Abuja, Nigeria, he snuck his family out of Bangassou in the back of a neighbor's milk-truck. Oscar and his family waited at the airport for there flight to come in, the day Oscar and his family came out of the airplane in Abuja a tremendous weight came off his shoulders (a weight of safety for his family), he could now provide a safe place for his family to live.

On Sunday afternoon after church Oscar came home with his family, this was his relaxing-time he would use this time and go to the backyard where he had a greenhouse and tend to his plants, giving them loving by singing to them and giving them his undivided attention. He grew various types of tropical plants Elephant Ear, Canna Lilly, Bromeliad, Dumb Canes etc... After Oscar tended to his plants he would sit on a lawn-chair in the greenhouse and read a novel while sipping on a rock-glass half full of Appleton Estate Rhum. This Sunday wasn't any different, Oscar sat there reading his novel when a mailman from Personal Express came into the greenhouse to hand him a parcel. Oscar went to stand up out of his seat to see if there was anything he had to sign, that's when the man took out of his shirt a hand-gun with a silencer on it and shot Oscar four times in the chest. After shooting Oscar the man took off, a few minutes went by and Oscar's son Jeffery came out to the greenhouse to ask his dad for change to buy candy at the corner store, that's when he saw his dad slumped over in his chair dead, Jeffery cried out for his mother.

August 18th 2022, Alan's Landing, Janoesha Harbour

After the Harbour Fair and the celebration of the island's discovery things started to slow down and people got back to their familiar routine. In Alan's Landing President Myers held a press conference outside at Jordan Square, Jason Umaumbaeya RC Elect for Merton Region was with him along with the Director Of Recreation for Janoesha Harbour Debra Gbeho and three JBI agents acting as security. A nice size crowd formed at the Square, President Myers was thanking Debra and the people of Janoesha Harbour for making this years Gala Star and Harbour Fair a success. President Myers gave Debra a bouquet of Janoesha Harbour's national flower the Showy Medinilla, he also placed a blue first place ribbon to the city around her neck, there were cheers and applause from the crowd as he did so, he kissed her on the cheek "okay I believe everyone would like to hear a word from the Director Of Recreation" Sterling said to her. As Debra went to say something to the crowd a bullet pierced through the daytime sky that nobody heard leave the gun with the sound as a whisper in the night, it hit Jason Umaumbaeya between the eyes, the back of his head sprayed out in a red mist onto the JBI agent standing behind him. There was screams in the crowd as Jason's body fell to the ground "shots fired, shots fired" one of the JBI agents reported on his walkie-talkie as he pulled out his side-arm and pointed it to the sky in front of him not sure what direction the shot came from. The President's security rushed him out of the Square and into his limo, everyone in the crowd started running for cover, they were worried that more shots would be fired.

An hour later in Jwelles a suburb of Alan's Landing Jeff Acheampong a thirty-six year old Specialist out of Nigeria was sitting on the bed inside a motel-room he had rented for the night. He was taken apart a .300 Winchester Magnum sniper rifle with silencer, he took it apart with ease and put the pieces in a large black briefcase he had opened up on his lap. Jeff closed up the briefcase and slid it under the bed, he then turned on the laptop that was on the bed beside him, on its screen was a information-sheet on Jason Umaumbaeya. On the top right hand corner of the sheet was the number four million in digits, Jeff clicked on it with his cersur and the number was transferred as money into one of his overseas accounts. After doing that another information-sheet came up on the screen, this one was on Moses Uatobuu, altogether Jeff had three information-sheets. Early in the morning around 4am Jeff loaded his gear into his 2021 grey GMC SUV and headed out to a remote cabin in north Pearles, sort of a safe-house arranged by his employer. It took him just under an hour on Highway 32 to get to the cabin, he had to make a stop in central Tamerra. The fridge in the cabin was stocked with food and the kitchen cupboards were filled with plates and glasses. The cabin was located in the dense woods but not quite in the Black Forest Region.

They doubled security at the Orange Gate and at President Myers house in Martin's Grove, just before 11am at the Orange Gate President Myers was in his chambers speaking with Defense Minister Walt Buyer and four star general David Bankole about the incident that happened at Jordon Square "where are we at with this" President Myers asked the two men with a sound of concern in his voice "I have JBI agents combing the Square for any spent casings" Walt informed him. "Sir just let me know what you want me to do" David said to President Myers "right now we have no clue who killed Jason so there's not much you can do" President Myers replied. President Myers looked down at his desk thinking on the next step to take, he then looked at Walt "Walt let me know what you get from the sweep of the Square, I'm going to arrange Jason's funeral" President Myers informed the two men as he stood up from behind his desk "General I'll get back to you when I've obtained more information on this matter" President Myers said to David before he left the room.

Walt Buyer went back to his office at the Orange Gate, he sat behind his desk thinking on what happened at Jordan Square 'why would someone shoot Jason Umaumbaeya' he thought to himself "maybe to get at someone" he answered himself 'could this be directed at the President' he thought more into it. Just to be safe Walt decided on treating this as a terrorist threat, he got Homeland Security to check the airports for all flights coming in for the pass two days. Walt got on the phone and called a friend he knew that worked for Airport Security at Crystal International "hello, hey Steve how you doing" Walt spoke into the phone "hey

I was wondering if you could check something for me" he asked Steve "can you check all flights coming in on August 17 at night" Walt asked "thank you" he then replied to Steve. Walt was on hold for no more than ten minutes, Steve came back with some good information, he told Walt that a standby flight from Nnamdi Azikiwe International Airport in Abuja, Nigeria came into Crystal International at 1:12am on August 18th, he also told him through a security check of one of the tickets, seat 42 on that flight was occupied by forty year old Company Welder Emerson Adomako, his ID showed he had a Ghanaian address. Steve informed Walt that the information that they had on Emerson Adomako was all fake, he was not a welder from Ghana "maybe a security-camera cot an image of this guy" Walt said to Steve "Okay check all security recordings around that time" Walt told Steve "let me know what you find, oh and Steve we're on high alert the Presidents life is at threat here" Walt told him and hung up the phone.

August 20th 2022, Tamerra, Janoesha Harbour

Moses and Stacey bought a starter-home, a small two bedroom bungalow in the Bluewinds neighborhood of southern Tamerra. Moses was in the garage tightening up the bolts on his truck's tires with a vice grip while drinking a Blue Toucan, the truck's radio was on, the sounds of a Kelo-Ball match was heard throughout the garage and down the driveway. Moses finished his bottle of beer and chucked the empty bottle in the garbage, he went to the beer-fridge he had in the garage to grab another bottle. Moses twisted the cap off the cold bottle of beer and flicked it out onto the driveway, Stacey didn't like him doing that but he did anyway behind her back. The garage wasn't attached to the house so Moses made it his own man-cave/mental escape from everything, a place where he can work and think, he was in the process of installing a surveillance hub in there. Stacey called out to Moses from the front door, Moses turned down his truck's radio "YES HON" he replied "I HAVE TO SHOW YOU SOMETHING" she told him, Moses turned off the radio and left the garage as he did so he closed down the garage door and headed inside the house. Moses took off his shoes inside the front door and went to the kitchen where he thought Stacey was but she wasn't, she was sitting on the couch in the living room watching the TV. Moses saw her and came up next to her "what's up honey" he asked her "the RC Elect for Merton Region was assassinated two days ago" she informed him as she pointed at the TV. Moses looked at the TV, the news was reporting live from Jordan Square, the lady on the news said that the JBI is looking for any spent casings in or around the Square and asking people questions on what they saw that day, she also said that the Immigration, Security & Defense Service is looking at this as a threat on the island whether domestic or foreign. "Someone shot Jason" Moses said to no one in particular "you know the person who was shot" Stacey asked as she turned and looked up at Moses standing next to her "yeah his name is Jason Umaumbaeya, I met him a couple times in the past through Ex-General Banes, who would want to kill him" Moses replied. "Do you think this is connected to what happened two years ago" Stacey asked Moses "I don't think so, Jason had nothing to do with that" Moses replied. The news was over, it was the morning news that ran for a half an hour from 10am to 10:30am, Stacey stood up out of the couch and kissed Moses on the mouth "well I've got to get ready I'm going to the news-station" she told Moses as she headed to the bedroom "I was kind of hoping we would get a bite to eat before you do so" Moses said to her following closely behind her while gently squeezing her butt and kissing the back of her neck. Stacey giggled as she tried to getaway from his touch "honey no I can't I gotta go to work" she told him as she got away from his grasp and locked herself in the washroom "no fare, poor sport" Moses said in a pouty voice, he went back to the living room and sat on the couch.

Alan's Landing, Janoesha Harbour

Walt had just gotten out of a meeting with the head of immigration and security with ISD, Walt had agreed to bring in Janoesha Harbour's Immigration, Security & Defense Service otherwise known on the island as (ISD) Immigration, Security & Defense. ISD agents wear grey-army fatigue with a black Kevlar-vest and a white band around their right arm that says ISD in bold black letters, the side-arms they carry is a Walther P99 and a roll of flex-cuffs, they also hold a light machine-gun an AR-15, their duties are to guard the airports and harbours from any terrorist entry and to protect the country from a terrorist takeover or threat. The president signed off on the injunction to bring the ISD into the investigation in who shot Jason Umaumbaeya. Walt got a call on his cell-phone from Steve at Crystal International "hey Steve what's up" Walt answered the phone "we found a recording, how soon can you get here" Steve asked him "I'm on my way there right now, what is the recording of" Walt asked him "one of our surveillance-cameras in Gate/Entrance 12 captured a black man coming in the airport off of flight 220 departure from Nnamdi Azikiwe Airport in Nigeria on August 18th" Steve informed him. While Walt was on the phone with Steve he was in the underground garage of the Orange Gate walking to his car. It took Walt about fifteen minutes to get to the airport, there was ISD agents guarding the entrance of the airport. Walt parked his car at the front entrance, he opened the door, got out and headed up to the airport's front doors. He was met by an ISD agent at the door "I'm gonna need to see some identification" the agent told Walt as he stood in front of his path holding a machine-gun, Walt showed him his government credentials "sorry sir continue on" the agent said as he stepped aside so Walt could get by. Walt headed to Gate/Entrance 12 where Steve was waiting for him, even though Crystal International is a huge airport it didn't take Walt too long to find Gate/Entrance 12. As Walt got to the gate he could see that Steve was there with someone from Homeland Security and two ISD agents "hey how you doing" Steve said as he shook Walt's hand "pretty good, lets see this recording" Walt replied "follow me" Steve told Walt, they went into a security-room just left of Gate/Entrance 12, the two ISD agents stood guard outside the door. There were three security-monitors in the room, on one of the monitors Steve played the recording for Walt and paused it when the camera cot a good image of the man "my people at Homeland Security have identified the individual in this recording" Len O'Donnell Informations Analysis for Homeland Security told Walt "who is he" Walt asked Len "he's thirty-six year old Jeffery Adwin Acheampong, born May 28th 1985 in the Central African Republic, his military background says his rank is a Gunnery Sergeant, he served twelve years in the Nigerian Army Special Forces, it says that he left the army with a Badge Of Honor" Len told him and continued as he pointed to the monitor "look at his right hand, he's holding some kind of briefcase that I found out wasn't checked out at customs" he said to Walt and Steve "that can easily conceal a rifle" Steve said "we have to find this man before anyone else gets hurt" Walt said "we should make sure that the police is on alert for this guy" Len said to Walt "yes that doesn't sound like a bad idea" Walt replied.

Tamerra, Janoesha Harbour

After Stacey left for work Moses decided that he would look into who shot Jason Umaumbaeya being that he had nothing else better to do, he was off from work for the next month and a half, that's when the next building-contract gets signed by the company that contracts him. Moses drove his pickup truck to where Ex-General Banes is doing time, at a military prison named Ollie on Base Laysan, they couldn't send the ex-general to Greystone because he's responsible for a portion of those prisoners being locked up there. It took Moses just under a half an hour to drive to the prison on base, military-police at Base Laysan knew Moses from his previous services in the army but he still had to show his ID at the gate "welcome to Base Laysan Captain" the MP said to him as he opened the gate. Moses drove onto the base and made a right turn at the first street, that street lead him in a half arch to the front of Ollie A Military Jail the sign read over the front entrance of the large grey-stone building, Ollie Jail was called a jail but it was like a prison, there is some pretty twisted and heinous people spending time there even though it's not as big as Greystone. Moses parked his truck out front, he got out and shot the door, heading up the large concrete steps of the building to its front doors. Moses pushed open the large mahogany-door and went in, he walked down a short hallway to the Warden's office that was on the left, Moses knocked on the door "come in" he heard a voice say from behind the door, Moses opened the door and went in. The warden was sitting behind a desk talking on the phone, he motioned to Moses that it was okay for him to take a seat, Moses sat down in one of the two chairs that were in front of the desk. After a few minutes the warden hung up the phone "how can I help you sir" the warden asked Moses with a smile "I'm here to see Terrance Banes" Moses replied "aw yeah the general, you must be Moses" the warden said as he looked at the visitor's list on the desk in front of him "yes sir I am" Moses replied "please call me Stanley" the warden told Moses as he grabbed a bunch of keys out of the top drawer of his desk "okay Stanley" Moses said "come on follow me" Stanley told him as he got up from behind his desk and left the office, Moses followed behind him. Stanley escorted Moses down a long hallway and across the yard of the prison (what they call the general population area) to a set of doors that opened up to another hallway, they walked down the short hallway to a steel-door on their right. Stanley opened up the cell-door with a large steel-key "you have a half an hour, when you're done press the black-button on the small metal panel on the wall beside the door" Stanley told him "thank you" Moses said to him and went in. It was a 14 feet by 10 feet cell with black padded walls and a polished concrete floor, the cell was furnished with a bed a night-table in one corner and a sink and toilet in another corner, there was a small TV on the night-table. Ex-General Banes was sitting in a wheel-chair in the middle of the cell "why it's the Captain, here to gloat" Banes said sarcastically to Moses "I'm here to ask you some questions" Moses replied "are you sure you're not here to kill me" Banes continued with his sarcastic tone "yes I'm sure" Moses replied "I mean look at me, it wouldn't take much to finish the job" Banes said "you only have yourself to blame for this" Moses told him "so you are here to gloat" Banes said to Moses "no really I'm not" Moses assured him. "If not to gloat then what" Banes asked him "the RC Elect for Merton Region was killed" Moses told him "Jason Umaumbaeya, are you sure" Banes asked surprise to hear the news "yeah I'm sure it's all over the news" Moses replied, Banes looked up at Moses "what does that have to do with me" Banes asked him. Moses looked down at the Ex-general not too sure if he could ever be trusted again "I want to know if this has anything to do with what happened two years ago" Moses asked him sternly "quite possible a lot of lives were lost that day" Banes replied "could Jessepi be behind this" Moses inquired "that is also possible, he does have connections in Cuba and Africa" Banes replied "what do you mean" Moses asked "Jessepi is a Large Game Hunter for a place called

The Farm in Cuba, their hunters are sent all over the world on different hunting expeditions, Jessepi did well in central and western Africa he gained a lot of respect there and made friends in high places" Banes informed him "do you think he would seek revenge" Moses asked Banes "well you did kill his whole crew and men like that don't like to be made a fool of" Banes replied. When Moses finished speaking with Ex-General Banes he left Base Laysan and headed back to Tamerra on Highway 32 "so this might be related to what happened two years ago" Moses said to himself as he drove north on Highway 32. He exited off the highway at Route 36 and got onto Route 54 heading north, he was planning on stopping off at his favorite bistro at Route 25 for a bite to eat. It didn't take him that long to get to Route 25, the bistro was at the corner of Route 54 & 25 it was named Gale's Bistro, they had a group of round white-metal tables with umbrellas through the center of them and four fancy black-chairs around each of them outside in front of the bistro, there was a black-steel fence surrounding the tables, mounted on the fence were small decorative lights shaped like water and palm-trees. Moses parked his truck on Route 54 and headed to the Gale's, when he got to Gale's Bistro he sat down around one of the tables, there was a middle aged lady sitting at the table across from him she looked like the executive type to Moses 'probably an accountant' Moses thought, she was drinking a large mug of gourmet coffee and typing in her Mac-Book. A young couple that looked to be in their early twenties came in beyond the fence and was currently walking by the table Moses was sitting around heading to the front counter of the bistro, Moses was waiting for a waitress, he got up out of his seat to look to see how much money he had in his wallet he counted forty-five rupees, as he sat back down a bullet that wasn't heard missed the top of his head by two inches and hit the young man with his girlfriend in the temple standing behind him, the other side of the young man's head sprayed out in a red mist filled with little chunks of brain and skull all over his girlfriend's face and hair, his girlfriend let out a blood-curdling scream as she watched her boyfriend's body collapse to the ground. Moses turned around at the sound of the scream and saw a dead body on the ground, another silent shot shattered the bistro's display-window, people were running for cover, Moses ducked down and ran into the bistro, he went into the washroom because he knew he was going to change into Silverback, the transformation took about eight minutes. Silverback came crashing up through the ceiling and landed on the roof of the bistro, he started beating his chest and began jumping from roof to roof another bullet just missed him as he was in mid flight jumping from a barber shop roof onto the side of the Janoesha Savings & Loans Tower. Silverback had pin-pointed where the shots were coming from, he grabbed his sword and whip out of the back of his truck, he didn't have his shield that was in a cave at Crest Climb in the Turynfoymus Mountains. The shots came from the roof of the WD Sugar Building three blocks away, when Silverback got there he saw that there was no one there only a tan-ghillie suit and a plastic-bottle of urine.

Jeff saw through the scope of his rifle that it was an ape jumping from roof to roof, he wasn't all that surprised, he was expecting something like this if he missed and he did.

Jeff could see the ape jumping to a taller building closer to where he was, he took another shot at the ape and missed, the bullet went under the ape's right arm, Jeff immediately took off his ghillie-suit and tossed it aside, he then took apart his rifle and put it in the briefcase. Jeff opened the door to the roof of the building and headed downstairs to the main-floor, he was moving at a comfortable pace as not to alert anyone, when he got to the main-floor he exited the building through the front door. Outside the WD Sugar Building Jeff got into his SUV, he put the briefcase on the front passenger-seat, started up the SUV and sped away. He was heading back to Pearles 'Moses earned a reprieve, I will try again another day' Jeff thought to himself as he turned right onto Route 23 that went east into Pearles. Jeff's cabin was located ten minutes north in the Ormetha Hills a suburban neighborhood of Pearles and just south of the Black Forest. There is a lot of dense palm in the Ormetha Hills, all kinds of different types of palm-trees, Date palms, Howea forsterianas, Roystonea regia and Sabal Palms are all up in the hills with many more plant-life. Jeff turned left onto Route 62 when he got into Pearles, he took it north into the Ormetha Hills and then turned right onto Route 19. On Route 19 he stopped off at a Village Opening to pick up a pack of smokes and something to eat, the Village Opening looked like it was a small church in a past-life, only converted into a store within the past fifty years. Jeff parked his SUV in the parking lot that was in front of the store and went in, it didn't take him long to find what he was looking for, he bought a pack of Green Peak cigarettes and a foot long roast beef sub with a large bottle of natural spring-water. Jeff left the Village Opening and got into his

SUV, he exited the parking lot and got back onto Route 19 heading west. While on Route 19 Jeff's disposable cell-phone started ringing on the dashboard, Jeff looked at the incoming number, it was an overseas number, he answered it "yes" he said in a soft voice "did you complete the contract" a male voice asked him "two left" Jeff replied not changing his tone "get it done" the male voice told him and hung up on his end, Jeff hung up the phone and threw it out the open window. He turned left onto Route 63 and started driving north to his cabin, he saw lots of different animals come out of the woods onto the gravel shoulder of the road as he drove along Route 63 like, Okapis, Nubian goats, Sambar deers, Hog deers and Alpacas, they would feed on the different berries and leaves that grew on the bushes that were along the shoulder of the road. The ground was dry around the Black Forest this time of year causing a lot of dust to build up in the air as the SUV made its way up an incline towards the cabin. The cabin was located just off Route 63 on a small escarpment of rock surrounded by a grove of Sabal Palm-trees, African tulip trees and Mahogany-trees. There were no paved roads near and around the cabin, this time of year in the hills looked like a drought with the hot August Janoesian sun beaming its rays down on everything, but the plant life still maintained their plush-green look. Jeff pulled into the driveway of the cabin, he grabbed his briefcase off the front passenger seat and exited the SUV, he headed up the wooden steps of the cabin to the front door. Jeff opened the door and went in, it was a one bedroom cabin with kitchen and full living room & bathroom, the cabin was built of stone and its roof of mahogany logs. Inside there were pictures hung on walls in the living room and in the hallway leading to the bathroom, in the living room there was a brown sofa and a center piece table, across from the sofa was a flat-screen TV sitting on a black TV stand, Jeff put the briefcase on the sofa and sat down beside it, he stretched his arms and shoulders out of tension and started eating his sub and drinking his bottle of spring-water.

Alan's Landing, Janoesha Harbour

Walt had been back at the Orange Gate for the last two hours after meeting with Steve at Crystal International, he was behind his desk going through some unrelated paperwork when his phone started ringing, he answered it, it was Major Joe Anhime head of the ISD, he informed Walt that there has been another shooting in Tamerra, twenty year old Kennedy Grant was shot in the head "a civilian" Walt asked him "yes sir" Joe replied "this is bad, very bad" Walt told Joe "I know sir" Joe agreed "okay shut off a three block radius so the JBI can search for evidence" Walt instructed him "there's one more thing sir, one of my men recovered a bullet out front of Gale's Bistro, he told me it looks to be from a .300 Winchester Magnum sniper-rifle" Joe informed him "good work" Walt said to Joe and hung up the phone. 'So it was a contract hit on Jason' Walt thought to himself 'but why kill a civilian' Walt thought into it, questioning the sequence of events "he's not finish" he said to himself. Walt picked up a black TV remote from off his desk and turned on the flat-screen TV that was mounted on the wall to the right of him, he surfed through the channels until he found a news channel. On the TV it showed journalist Janet Jacobson from TJNX News reporting live from Gale's Bistro out in Tamerra "an hour and a half ago there was a shooting outside this bistro, the police are drawing a blank coming up with a motive behind the shooting, all they know is that twenty year old Geology student at the University Of Janoesha Harbour in Umni Kennedy Alex Grant was shot in the head and died at the scene, his traumatize girlfriend was brought to Tamerra Memorial Hospital" Janet reported and continued "witnesses to the shooting say they saw a large ape-like creature jump off the roof of a barber-shop and onto the side of the Janoesha Savings & Loans tower, is this a repeat of two years ago" she asked their viewers. Walt immediately thought of Moses and then called Joe back "hello Joe, it's Walt, did you check any vehicles near the bistro" he asked Joe "yeah we searched a Ford pickup that was parked on Route 54 beside the bistro, I ran the license-plate and it came back Captain Moses Uatobuu" Joe informed him "inform the JBI about this and make sure no one touches that pickup" Walt instructed him "yes sir, may I ask why" Joe said to him "because I think the killer is working off a list" Walt replied.

Tamerra, Janoesha Harbour

Silverback hid out from the press in a patch of woods behind the Space Lab until he turned back into his normal self, Moses body was getting use to the transformation, he didn't experience anymore cold-sweats or fevers. Moses covered up himself with an old brown potato-sack he found in the woods, he walked out to Route 50 and eventually flagged down a cab, the cab-driver was surprise to see a man standing on the side of the road wearing a potato-sack, he wondered how this person was going to pay him. The blue and white cab stopped in front of Moses, the front passenger-side window came down "I don't do charity here sir" the driver told Moses "I live in the Bluewinds neighborhood I can pay you when we get there" Moses told him, the driver knew the Bluewinds area 'a lot of rich people live out there' he thought to himself and then decided to take Moses where he wanted to go. "Come on in" the cab-driver motioned to Moses as he unlocked the back- door for him, Moses opened the door and slid into the back-seat, he shot the door as he got comfortable, the cab-driver sped off heading south on 50 "I can give you a flat rate of 60 rupees" the driver said to Moses "whatever is comfortable with you" Moses replied still thinking about what just happened to him, he was planning on going home to get dress and then heading back to the bistro to pick up his truck. It took the cab-driver forty minutes to get to the Bluewinds neighborhood, the cab drove up Moses driveway, stopped and parked "I won't be long" Moses told the driver as he opened up the back-door and got out, he headed up to the front door of his house and lifted up the brown rug that was on the small front patio. Moses picked up the key that was under the rug and opened the front door, he went in and headed down the hall to the kitchen, in a drawer beside the sink he had some cash (three hundred rupees to be exact), he took 65 rupees and went back to the cab, the cab-driver was answering another fare that came over his UHF radio "yes I'm about five minutes away" he told dispatch and hung up. Moses came around to the open driver's side window "here you go, thank you very much for the ride" he told the driver as he handed him the cash, the driver gave him a honest smile and backed out of his driveway. Moses went back in his house, closed the door and headed to the bathroom to take a shower, he got out of the itchy potato-sack and turned on the shower. He stepped into the lukewarm shower and with a rag and soap started washing off the violent-grime he could smell on his body, smoke and sweat, somethings he's trying his best to stay clear of, he made a promise to Stacey that he will never go back to his old life as a soldier, they were going to get married soon and start a life together. When Moses finished rinsing the soap off his body he turned off the shower and stepped out of its glass-cage, he grabbed a towel off the towel-rack and put it around his waist, making his way to the bedroom he started drying off himself with the towel. Moses sat naked on the bed as he went through a drawer in his dresser for clean underwears, he picked out one that was grey with purple stripes, Moses put on the underwear and went over to the closet, at the closet he grabbed a pair of blue-jeans and a grey button-up shirt with fancy black-buttons.

Pearles, Janoesha Harbour

Jeff was watching the TV as he went through the kill-list he had on his lap-top, he was reading through Moses Uatobuu's information-sheet, the TV was on Channel 8 boardcasting the news, journalist Rich Kessler was reporting live from the TJNX news station in Tamerra. "After the tragedy that happened at the Space Lab two years ago construction has started to re-build the historical landmark, in other news authorities still don't have any leads in the shooting at Gale's Bistro, there has been a fund put together by the people in the neighborhood where young Kennedy Grant use to live for the Grant family" Rich Kessler reported. 'In war there are always casualties' Jeff thought to himself as he looked at the TV screen, he turned off the TV and turned his attention back to the information-sheet on his lap-top, it said that Captain Moses Uatobuu did two tours in Afghanistan and left the army with an honorable discharge, it also said that he is highly advanced in close quarters combat. With Moses Jeff knew that he needed an edge, he also knew that for three and a half years Moses has been dating a crime-journalist named Stacey Lane, maybe that's the edge that he needs. Jeff took another disposable-phone out of his briefcase and made a call "I need information on a Stacey Lane" he said into the phone "you'll have it in five minutes" a voice on the other end said and hung up, Jeff hung up the phone and with both his hands broke it in two and tossed it into the small garbage-can that was next to the couch. After reading through Stacey Lane's information he packed up his briefcase and lap-top and headed out, he was going to Stage Park Theater to pick up a parcel. Stage Park Theater in Pearles is actually an outdoor stadium where live musical concerts and live comedy acts are performed, it's also the home to the Kelo-ball team Pearles Caimans, it is located in downtown Pearles at Route 64 & 25. Jeff drove down Route 63 to Route 24, when he got to Route 24 he turned left towards Route 64. It didn't take him long to get to Stage Park Theater, he parked his SUV outside the stadium under a Royal poinciana tree, there are several food kiosks outside Stage Park Theater, it also has some telephone kiosks outside the front door. Jeff was giving instructions to pick up a parcel out of one of the telephone kiosks, lucky for him it was late in the day and there wasn't anyone around the stadium this time of the day. The instructions were that there was a parcel left in kiosk number 6 to pick up, Jeff spotted kiosk number 6 next to the front door, he went over and retrieved the parcel. Jeff went back to his SUV and put the parcel on the back-seat, he started up the SUV and headed back to the cabin.

Alan's Landing, Janoesha Harbour

At the Orange Gate Walt Buyer was in the president's chambers with President Myers "we have a suspect in the assassination of Jason Umaumbaeya his name is Jeff Acheampong an ex-soldier out of Nigeria, he was cot on a security-camera at Crystal International" Walt informed President Myers "is that it" President Myers asked him. Walt sat up in his chair that was in front of president's desk "no, we believe that he's working off of a kill-list, we also know that the shooting that happened at Gale's Bistro wasn't random, he missed his target" Walt replied "what do you mean" President Myers inquired "we ran the license-plate of a pick-up truck that was parked beside the bistro, it came back belonging to a Captain Moses Uatobuu, there were also sightings of a large ape-like creature on the side of the Janoesha Savings & Loans Tower" Walt informed President Myers "if Moses is in danger we need to let him know"

President Myers told Walt and continued. "So that means this man was hired by someone" President Myers asked Walt "we believe so" Walt replied "do we know who" the president inquired "not yet but we will" Walt replied "could this be retaliation for what happened two years ago" President Myers asked concerned for Moses safety "quite possible, I'm not sure yet but I will find out" Walt replied. Walt stood up out of his chair and shook President Myers hand "thank you Walt for keeping me in the loop" the president said to him, Walt bowed his head in front of President Myers in sign of respect before he left his chambers. On the way back to his office Walt gave Moses a call on his cell-phone "hello" Moses answered "good evening Captain it's Defense Minister Walt Buyer at the Orange Gate" Walt replied "hi sir how can I help you" Moses asked him "where are you right now" Walt asked him "I'm in my pick-up heading home" Moses replied. "Tell me where you live and I'll send two ISD agents there" Walt told Moses "ISD agents, what's this about" Moses asked surprised about what Walt was saying "you might be in danger" Walt told him "what are you talking about" Moses inquired. Walt explained it to him "a suspect in the shooting of Jason Umaumbaeya was cot on a security-camera at Crystal International, through our investigation we found out that he is an ex-soldier for the Nigerian Army Special Forces, we believe he's working off a kill-list" Walt said "what does that have to do with me" Moses asked Walt "his rank in the Nigerian Special Forces is Gunnery Sergeant, he's an ex-sniper" Walt told him. Moses didn't say anything for a bit, Walt thought the line went dead "hello, hello" Walt said into the phone "how did he get pass Customs Police" Moses asked him "he used a fake ID" Walt replied "yeah but how did he get his luggage through, CP Officers always check all hand carried luggage" Moses inquired "we're looking into that" Walt assured him "there must be a person on the inside that helped him get into the country" Moses told Walt 'he has a point' Walt thought to himself "I live at 3741 Bluewinds Circle" Moses told him "okay I'll send two agents over" Walt told Moses and hung up. Walt was thinking about what Moses said about an inside source so he decided on doing a soft investigation into the Customs Police starting with Crystal International Airport. Customs Police (CP) otherwise known on the island as a CP Officer, CP Officers work at customs in the airports and at the International Ports, their jobs are to check all luggages for any illegal drugs or weapons and to dispose of all restricted foods brought into the country, CP Officers carry on them pepper-spray and side-arms, a Sig Sauer P320 and a pair of handcuffs.

Tamerra, Janoesha Harbour

It took Moses thirty minutes to get home from going back for his pick-up at Gale's Bistro, the Feds didn't give him a hard time, they just asked for ID, a couple of those JBI boys looked familiar to Moses, quite possible they could of served with him overseas way back when. Moses drove up onto his driveway, there were two ISD agents standing out front of his house "damn that was fast" Moses said to himself, Moses parked his truck in the garage, his sword and whip were in the pick-up. When he exited the garage he pulled down the garage-door and walked over to one of the ISD agents "hi how you doing, Walt said you were coming by" Moses said to the agent as he extended his hand in friendship, they shook hands "yes Captain we're here twenty-four seven for you, we have a surveillance van parked across the street" the agent informed Moses "please call me Moses, if there's anything you guys need don't hesitate to ask" Moses told the agent and then left for the front door. Moses opened the front door to his house and went in, he could see that Stacey was home, she was in the kitchen making a salad, it was actually a Sweet Potato & Avocado Green Salad, she made two plates. "This is the latest you came home since we lived together" Moses said to her as he came up from behind and hugged her, they kissed "how was your day hon" she asked Moses "it's best I tell you later" Moses replied "I met up with Carol at Cuddle Friendly's, we went to look at dresses for bride-maids" Stacey told him. Stacey rested the two plates of salad on the kitchen-table "you must be hungry" she said to Moses.

Alan's Landing, Janoesha Harbour

Early the next day around 8:30am at the Orange Gate President Myers called a meeting with Defense Minister Walt Buyer, PC Elect for Passco Region Erik Spencer, Federal Energy Director Charles McFarlen and PC Elect for Edward Region Genesee Lockport. The meeting was held in the Gate's courtyard, surrounded by dense ivy hedging and nostalgic marble-statues of past dignitaries, standing on a ground of neatly cut St. Augustine grass is President Myers and the rulers of Janoesha Harbour. The meeting was to swear in Alvin Powers as new Regional Commander for Merton Region, Major Alvin Powers ran the police department in Alan's Landing for fourteen years until he took some time off to write true-crime novels, at the present time him and his wife of forty years and dog named Scout live in Spirit's Cove. Alvin Powers held up his right hand and placed his left hand on his heart and swore to up hold the Janoesian Constitution and to protect the Albatross of the Janoesian Seal (the Janoesian flag) at whatever cost from enemies whether foreign or domestic. President Myers swore in Alvin Powers as PC Elect for Merton Region, he placed a powdered-blue sash over Alvin's left shoulder and gave him a respectful hand-shake with both his hands. The inauguration took about fifteen minutes, everyone shook Alvin's hand and patted him on the shoulder congratulating him in his new position "there's cake in the dining room" President Myers announced. They all were now congregated in the Gate's large fancy dining room eating a piece of cake and enjoying a glass of champagne, while the others socialized amongst themselves and with the other staff President Myers and Walt Buyer had a conversation. "Anything new in the investigation" President Myers asked Walt "something Moses said inspired me to call the Central Hub for Customs Police at Crystal International, I found out that on the day Jeff Acheampong was cot on a security-camera a new CP Officer showed up for shift-change at Gate/Entrance 12, it wasn't the regular officer, another thing is the new CP Officer signed in as

Shane Eggerton and we haven't been able to locate him" Walt informed the president "do you have any information on him" President Myers inquired "right now I have Len O'Donnell looking into it" Walt replied "if there's a security-breach at the airport the press will have a field-day with it, get this under control Walt" President Myers told him "yes sir nothing to worry about everything is under control" Walt assured the president. "Good so how's the wife and kids" President Myers asked Walt and took a sip of his champagne "she's well, the kids are on a camping trip out by Hubber's Lake" Walt replied. President Myers knew Walt from when he was an Admiral for the Southern Royal Navy Fleet Of Janoesha Harbour (otherwise known as the Southern Royal Navy (SRN)), their ships are docked at Base Laysan and just north of Mollymawk Marina. Walt took another glass of champagne off the dining room table, he promised himself that it would be his last "one thing I forgot to mention that Len told me is that after Jeff was discharged from the army he worked as a Specialist in the Central African Republic the place of his birth, he would do whatever job paid well, usually working for political figures, his grandfather Lethabo Bwana Acheampong was in the Biafra War between 1967 and 1970, he drove tank" Walt informed President Myers "doesn't The Farm in Cuba send hunters to the Central African Republic" President Myers asked him "I'm not sure" Walt replied wondering how the president knew that "Frank found that out when he arrested Jessepi" the president told Walt "how is Sergeant Allister" Walt asked "he took some time off to visit his parents in Canada" President Myers informed Walt.

Tamerra, Janoesha Harbour

After Moses and Stacey ate their salads they sat in the living room to watch some TV and talk, Moses told her about his day and the shooting at Gale's Bistro. Stacey felt for him "I'm sorry to hear that happened to you love" Stacey told him as she gently rubbed his shoulder with her hand "did they find out who it was" she asked Moses "I'm not sure" he replied "I feel bad for that young man's family" Stacey said "yeah me to" Moses agreed. "Walt Buyer said that the shot that killed the kid was meant for me" Moses told Stacey "what, are you sure" Stacey asked Moses as she sat up straight in the couch no longer massaging Moses shoulder "yeah he said the shooter is working off a kill-list" Moses informed her "is that why those soldiers are out front, to keep us safe" Stacey questioned Moses "they're not soldiers they're ISD agents" Moses told her "well they look like soldiers to me" Stacey said "and yes they're here to keep us safe" Moses replied "we're getting married soon, we are planning on starting a family together" Stacey said to Moses "we can still do that" Moses replied. Stacey could see that there was something else on Moses mind, she took a guess "is this about Jessepi Montoya" she asked Moses, he couldn't maintain eye-contact when he answered her "I'm not sure yet" Moses replied "you can't even look at me when you say that, oh my God then it is a revenge thing" Stacey said in a worried tone as she covered her mouth with her hand "it might not be hon we just have to wait and see" Moses told her as he held her hands in his "I think I'm going to lay down for awhile" Stacey told Moses and got up and headed to the bedroom. Moses cell-phone started ringing, he answered it, it was Walt Buyer calling him from the Orange Gate "hello Walt how are you" Moses answered "not bad, so we found a breach in security with Customs Police, the CP Officer that works on that day didn't show up during shift change it was a new CP Officer, since then nobody has been able to find him" Walt informed Moses "so you think it was an inside job" Moses asked Walt "yes I do" Walt replied. Moses just remembered something "did the JBI check the roof of the WD Sugar Building" Moses asked Walt "no that's not within their search radius" Walt replied "have them search the roof of that building, that's where the shots came from" Moses told him.

Special Agent Chris Haddon head of the JBI's field office in Tamerra is leading the investigation into the shooting at Gale's Bistro, they had a three block radius to search in downtown Tamerra. They had already searched most of the stores and banks within the radius when Chris got a call on his cell-phone from Walt Buyer "Special Agent Haddon speaking" Chris answered "how's the investigation going" Walt asked him "slowly producing sir" Chris replied "have you checked the WD Sugar Building" Walt asked him already knowing the answer "that's outside the search radius sir" Chris told Walt "yeah I know but I just got a tip to search the roof of that building" Walt informed him "okay I'll send some men there right now" Chris told Walt. Walt hung up the phone on his end then Chris hung up, Chris sent five of his men to search the WD Sugar Building, taking point was Special Agent Shawn Morris.

They stormed into the front door of the WD Sugar Building with their guns drawn, ordering the employees and people that were in there to head outside, it took them awhile to search all thirty-eight floors of the building. On the staircase leading to the roof they found a bullet belonging to a .300 Winchester Magnum sniper-rifle, Shawn put the bullet in an evidence-bag and headed up to the roof. The door leading out to the roof was ajar, Shawn carefully pushed it open still with his gun drawn, he walked out onto the roof followed by four agents. On the roof Shawn saw a Ghillie-suit and a couple spent-casings from a .300 Winchester Magnum sniper-rifle "oh yeah here we go, jackpot" Shawn said as he stooped down to get a better look at the casings, he radioed into Chris "looks like we got a sniper boss" Shawn informed Chris "okay collect what you can and see if you can get any information off the employees, good job agent" Chris told him. Chris called back Walt on his cell-phone "hello Walt Buyer speaking" Walt answered "yep there was definitely someone on the roof of the WD Sugar Building" Chris told him "what did you find" Walt asked him "we found a Ghillie-suit and a couple spent-casings from a .300 Winchester Magnum sniper-rifle" Chris told Walt.

Jwelles, Janoesha Harbour

Officer Davis for Alan's Landing Police was responding to a call at a truck-stop in Jwelles, an employee at the truck-stop called the police about a body in a dumpster. Officer Davis wasn't too far from the truck-stop, when he got there the employee met him out front of the truck-stop. He got out of his cruiser and went up to where the employee was waiting "hi you called about a body in a dumpster" he said to the truck-stop employee, she dropped the cigarette that she was smoking on the ground and butted it out under her shoe "yeah it's right over here" she told the officer still a little shooking up from what she saw. "Before that can I get your name mam" Officer Davis asked her as he took a pen and writing-pad out of his shirt pocket "Jillian Rous" she replied "what's your birthday Jillian" Officer Davis asked her "April 5th 1987" Jillian replied "okay where's this dumpster" Officer Davis inquired. Jillian took Officer Davis around the left side of the truck-stop to a dark-blue dumpster, she kept her distance "it's right there officer" Jillian told him as she pointed to the dumpster "okay wait here" Officer Davis told her. Officer Davis walked up to the dumpster and opened up one of its hard black-plastic lids, he looked in and saw the dead body of a uniformed CP Officer. He called it into dispatch and they alerted the JBI, fifteen minutes later a group of JBI agents and a coroner's van showed up at the truck-stop. Special Agent Doug Fenwell and a medical examiner walked up to the dumpster with two assistants to the medical examiner, the assistants took the body out of the dumpster and put it in a black body-bag on a gurney, the corpse neck had been cut from ear to ear and it was missing its right hand. Before they zipped up the body-bag the M.E took a wallet out of the body's pants pocket and gave it to Doug, Doug opened it up and took a look at the ID inside, the ID read Shane Francis Eggerton born November 22nd 1973, he had a Brookshore address. Doug gave Walt a call "hello Walt Buyer speaking" Walt answered "hi sir it's Special Agent Doug Fenwell in Jwelles, it looks like we found Shane Eggerton" he told Walt "have you questioned him" Walt asked Doug "well he's not saying much" Doug replied "what do you mean" Walt asked him "we found him dead in a dumpster at a truck-stop" Doug told him "who found him" Walt inquired "the officer on call said an employee at the truck-stop discovered the body" Doug informed Walt. "I need you to bring the employee to the field-office in downtown Alan's Landing for questioning" Walt told Doug "will do sir" Doug said and hung up his cell-phone. Jillian was standing beside Officer Davis next to his cruiser when Doug came up to them "hi are you the one that found the body" Doug asked Jillian "yes, I came out to dump some garbage when I saw him" she replied. Doug looked at Officer Davis then back at Jillian "what do you do here" Doug asked her "I work as a clerk slash cook" she told Doug, Doug looked at Officer Davis "I'm going to need to speak with her for a minute" he told the officer "sure thing" Officer Davis said. Doug escorted Jillian over to his car and had her sit in the back seat with the door open, he stood over her with his body leaned up against the open door "from what I gathered from the police officer you have no criminal record so don't worry you're not in any trouble" he assured Jillian "well that's good to know" Jillian replied "I just need to know if you seen anything that looked off here in the past few days" Doug asked her. Jillian thought for a few seconds "yeah two days ago there was a grey SUV parked out front here for most of the day, nobody got out of

it, it was just sitting there like it was waiting for someone"
she told Doug "do you know what make it was" Doug
asked her "I believe it was GMC" Jillian replied "did you
get the license's plate number" Doug inquired "no I was too
busy attending to customers" Jillian told him. Doug put the
pen and note-pad he was holding back on the dashboard
of his car "okay, do you mind coming to the JBI office
downtown" he asked Jillian "sure I guess so, I don't know
how much more I can help you" Jillian replied "I just have a
few more questions to ask you, don't worry once we're done
I'll drive you back here or home which ever you prefer" he
told her. Jillian put her feet inside the car and he shut the,
Doug then opened the front driver's side door and slid in
behind the steering-wheel, he started up the car and drove
out of the truck-stop's parking lot onto Cashbridge Road.

Pearles, Janoesha Harbour

Jeff was at a Village Opening in its coffee shop enjoying a
mug of hot gourmet coffee and a blueberry muffin, he was
watch a Kelo-ball match on the flat-screen TV that was
mounted on the wall in the coffee shop. The coffee shop is
an open concept, that means you can leave the coffee shop
and enter into the variety store without opening a door. Jeff
sat around a table sipping on his coffee thinking about his
next mark 'he would have to grab Stacey Lane when she's
on her way home from work' he thought to himself. Just
then a masked man came in the variety store and pointed
a .38 Revolver at the clerk's head demanding her to open
the safe that was behind the counter she was at. Jeff just

sat at the table watching what was going on and not saying anything, the masked man looked at the young clerk as she tried to open the safe "you better get that open real soon or I'm going to blow your head off" he told her, but she was so scared and nervous that her hands were shaking and she couldn't get it open. Eventually she did get it open and the masked man took the stack of cash that was inside and then left the store, the young clerk was on the ground leaned up against the safe crying, thankful to be alive. Jeff got up from around the table and headed outside to where he saw the masked man walking towards a brown van, the man took off his mask and stuffed it in his pants pocket. Jeff quickly walked up behind him "hey" Jeff said to him, the man stopped and turned around to face Jeff "what do you want" the man asked Jeff as he gripped his gun that was in a holster around his waist warning Jeff to back off "where did you get that cash" Jeff asked him referring to the stack of bills he was holding in his left hand "go fuck yourself pal" the man told Jeff and was about to turn around and continue on his way when Jeff pulled out his Beretta M9 that he had in a holster around his waist and shot the man between the eyes, the back of the man's head sprayed out in a red-mist of blood and pieces of skull & brain, he fell to the ground in a puddle of his own blood. Jeff picked up the stack of cash and brought it back to the clerk. In the Village Opening the clerk thanked Jeff but she didn't like the fact that he killed someone, she knew she would have to call the cops so she gave Jeff some time to leave before she did so.

Tamerra, Janoesha Harbour

Hoopoe Greenhills is a suburban neighborhood located in southeast Tamerra, mostly the working lower middle-class, young families and families with teenage kids live there. The neighborhood was mostly bungalows with a few semi-detached houses surrounded by modest foothills covered in finely knitted St. Augustine grass. It's where the Grant family lives, they recently lost their son Kennedy to a sniper's bullet, Kennedy's mom and dad Alice and Virgil Grant were at their place with the TJNX Channel 8 News crew getting prepared to say something on the air. In a couple hours they would bury Kennedy, Janet Jacobson clipped a small microphone onto both Alice and Virgil's shirt "there you go, they should hear you clearly now" she told the mourning couple. Alice had dried the tears that streamed down her cheeks and restrained her emotional state while she was on air "our son Kennedy was a fun and loving boy that liked to help people in need, he was in school studying to become a geologist and you took him from us" Alice said on air to the person that killed her son as she then covered her mouth with one hand and broken down in tears again, Virgil held her tight in his arms, comforting her as he kissed her on the head while she cried with her face buried in his chest.

Spirit's Cove, Janoesha Harbour

At Shearwater Run in Spirit's Cove a Single-engine Cessna was stopped by the ISD as it came into the dock, the pilot and co-pilot were taking into the Customs Office for questioning. Through searching the plane ISD agents found a duffle-bag full of stun-grenades, half a million dollars in British pound sealed air-tight in clear plastic and a passport for Taitung, Taiwan. The ISD took everything they found on the plane to storage where it could be inspected, Special Agent Gary Adcliff of the JBI was leading the investigation into the shooting of Jason Umaumbaeya and Kennedy Grant here in Spirit's Cove.

Shearwater Run is a Seaplane dock in Spirit's Cove, seaplanes and smaller planes like Cessnas land there to re-fuel. It also has a restaurant and a motel for visitors, most of its business comes from planes from main land Africa and media planes from local radio stations doing promotional runs.

Gary came into the Customs Office, the pilot of the Cessna was sitting at an empty desk in handcuffs with an ISD agent standing guard over him, his co-pilot was in a interviewing room with two other ISD agents. The pilot was a young Caucasian man in his mid-thirty with curly sandy-brown hair that touched his shoulders, he was wearing a blue baseball-cap that read K C in white letters on the front. Gary pulled up a chair in front of the pilot and sat down "what's your name sir" he asked the pilot "JT" the pilot replied "you're in a lot of trouble JT" Gary told him "sir I can explain" JT said to Gary "please do" Gary said "I was to fly here and stay overnight and then fly back with an empty plane, I wasn't told to meet anyone and I wasn't giving any names, all I was told was that the money would be in my account when I got back to Mauritania" JT told Gary "where exactly did you fly from" Gary asked him "from a hangar in

Rosso". "Do you know who happens to manage or own the hangar" Gary inquired "I'm not sure, I do know though that it's used a lot by hunters that go on overseas expeditions" JT replied. Gary knew JT was holding back something his story just sound too self-serving "who hired you JT" Gary asked "I don't know" JT replied "come on you yourself said they were going to put money in your account once you got back plus you don't just agree to fly a plane without knowing whats on board or who you're going to meet" Gary told him. JT knew he had to say something but he was afraid of retaliation, 'these people have a long reach internationally' he thought to himself, he hung his head down not saying anything just staring at the floor "well from what we found in that Single-engine Cessna out there you and your partner in there are looking at forty years each in Greystone" Gary told him "sit tight JT you're gonna be here awhile, until we write up the paperwork for your transfer" Gary added as he stood up out of his chair and patted JT on the shoulder. JT looked up at Gary about to leave him sitting there "sir I honestly don't know anything" he pleaded to Gary "you must know something" Gary said as he sat on the edge of the desk beside JT, JT hung his head back down "you don't know who these people are" he said to Gary without looking at him "are you the owner of the plane outside" Gary asked JT changing the question "no" JT replied in a low voice "okay we're getting somewhere now, who owns it" Gary asked him "I don't know" JT replied "heck I thought I'd give it a shot" Gary said sarcastically as he shrugged his shoulders "sir I wish I could help you but I can't" JT told him "NO! I think you're full of shit, I think you're too afraid to speak and you think saying nothing is going to keep you alive but it's not true, it will only make things worst" Gary told him. JT looked up at Gary "do you promise to keep my family safe" he asked Gary with a concern look in his eyes "yes if your family is being held captive we can get them to safety" Gary assured JT "they're being held at a ranch in Bethanien, Namibia" JT told him "okay, okay slow down explain it to me, who are they" Gary asked JT "they're called The Farm and they own the hangar in Rosso" JT told Gary. Gary took out a pen and writing-pad from his jacket pocket and started writing down the information JT was telling him "the ID in your wallet says your from Brookshore, how did your family get mixed up with this thing in Africa" Gary asked JT "me and my wife are Wildlife Photographers, we occasionally go out to Africa on safaris to take pictures for a local magazine out of Beryl Rado, one safari we decided on bringing Tiana our twelve year old daughter, during the safari we meet a gentleman named Ronald who invited us to his ranch slash mansion for dinner, when we got to the ranch I saw that there was a tall stone wall surrounding the ranch, when we got in the ranch they wouldn't let us leave and that was a year and a half ago, they knew I had my pilot's licenses so they told me to fly the plane here if I didn't do it they would kill my wife and daughter" JT explained it to Gary "the contents of the plane, who were they for" Gary asked JT "I don't know all I know is that an Avis-van was to come and pick them up" JT replied 'there is an Avis Rental Office next to the Customs Office' Gary thought to himself "okay JT I'm gonna have you speak with a friend of mine" Gary told him as he got on his cell-phone and called Walt Buyer.

BARK ADAM

Bark Adam is a Janoesian children fable about a little boy named Adam that was defiant to his parents rules, he kept leaving the house for the day and coming back in the evening before the sun went down, so his parents locked him in his room chained to the bed only wearing a short white t-shirt and sneakers. When his mom and dad came back in the room to spank his bare bottom for the third time he had escaped from his chains and jumped to his death through his bedroom window. Now adults tell little kids to stay out of the woods or Bark Adam will spank their bare bottom because that's where Adam went when he was away all day, the woods, spying on people behind trees and bushes while only wearing a small white t-shirt and sneakers with his plump round bare bottom exposed for all to see. The adults say Bark Adam lives in the woods, he wears a small skin-tight t-shirt and sneakers, he always looks like an eight year old boy and his plump round spankable bare bottom is all he's concerned about "it's too tender to be spanked" he tells people who spot him hiding, he hides behind trees and bushes spying on people waiting for the right time to smack or pinch them, he's quite bashful and rambunctious at the same time, would never get into a position where he's cornered, most of the time evading capture, but it's said that they've been times that he was cot by an adult and spanked on his bare bottom leaving him in tears rubbing his sore bottom.

Spirit's Cove, Janoesha Harbour

The phone rang a couple times "hello Walt Buyer speaking" Walt answered "hi sir it's Special Agent Gary Adcliff out here in Spirit's Cove, we've stopped a small plane and brought in the pilot and his co-pilot here at Shearwater Run, I've been speaking with the pilot and he has some pretty interesting stuff to say" Gary told Walt. "Are you with him right now" Walt asked Gary "yes he's right here, I thought you might want to hear these things from him" Gary replied, Walt agreed "okay put him on the line" Walt told Gary. Gary held the cell-phone to JT's ear "go ahead speak" Gary told JT "hi who am I speaking with" JT asked into the phone "this is Federal Defense Minister Walt Buyer and you are" Walt replied, there was a fifty second pause of silence "sounds like you got yourself into a bit of a pickle over there" Walt said breaking the silence "I had no choice" JT replied "okay I understand, maybe I can help" Walt said to JT "they have my wife and daughter" JT told Walt "who are they" Walt asked JT "they're an organization of corrupted government officials and wealthy poachers called The Farm and they have my family captive on a ranch in Bethanien, Namibia" JT replied "did you say The Farm" Walt asked JT "yes The Farm" JT repeated "sir where are you from" Walt asked JT "Brookshore, Janoesha Harbour" JT replied "is your family citizens of this country" Walt inquired "yes we're all born here" JT answered not to sure what Walt was getting at "that's good, can I get your name sir" Walt asked JT, there was a fifteen second pause of silence "James T Haddler, everyone just calls me JT" JT replied "okay sit tight JT I'll see what I can do" Walt told him. Gary got back on the line "hello Special Agent Adcliff speaking" Gary said "check him out, if he comes back clean we might be in position for an extraction" Walt told Gary "will do sir" Gary replied "good job agent" Walt said to Gary and hung up the phone on his end.

Alan's Landing, Janoesha Harbour

It was after 7pm and the sun was going down over the foothills in the distance, Walt was in his car heading home up Shore Street to the upscale suburb of Dichondra Briar, he's been living there in a three bedroom bungalow with his wife, fifteen year old son and eighteen year old daughter for the past ten years. Dichondra Briar is a suburb of Alan's Landing bordered to the west of the suburb of Rockridge, Dichondra Briar's neighborhood lawns are carpeted with Dichondra grass, I guess that's where they got the name from, it also grows very thick in the parks there. Walt got on his cell-phone and gave President Myers a call, the phone rang a few times and then the president picked up "hello President Sterling Myers speaking" the president answered. President Myers was still at the Orange Gate finishing up some important paperwork "hi sir it's Walt Buyer" Walt said "hey Walt, you must be heading home right now" President Myers replied to Walt "yes but that's not why I called" Walt told him "what's on your mind" President Myers asked Walt with a concerned tone in his voice "there might of been a break in the case of the shooting of Jason Umaumbaeya" Walt informed him "what do you mean" President Myers asked Walt "we might have found out who orchestrated this whole thing, I was speaking on the phone with a pilot that was taking to customs by the JBI for questioning at Shearwater Run in Spirit's Cove, he told me he was hired by an organization call The Farm and they have a ranch in Bethanien, Namibia" Walt told President Myers "I knew Jessepi had something to do with this, this is retaliation for two years ago" President Myers said "I'm not too sure it's just that" Walt said to President Myers "what else could it be" President Myers asked Walt "JBI said that the money found on the airplane was in British Pounds, the pound has very little worth here" Walt told the president "they also found a duffle-bag full of stun-grenades and a passport from Taitung, Taiwan" Walt added "who was that all for" President Myers asked Walt "just a hunch but I think the money and the grenades are to fund a hunt in the Black Forest, I'm guessing hunters from Europe will be participating, the passport is for Jeff Acheampong so he can get to The Farm's next hunt" Walt told President Myers. President Myers couldn't believe it "so there are two Farms" President Myers asked Walt "the way the pilot put it, it sounds like they are a well funded organization with political figures as members, they might have franchises all over the world but lets hope not, lets hope the only two are in Cuba and Namibia" Walt told President Myers "one other thing the pilot's from here and they have his wife and daughter hostage on a ranch in Namibia, they are both born here on Janoesha Harbour, I think we can sign off for an extraction" Walt added "okay call David if he's okay with it I'll sign off on it" President Myers told Walt "okay sir" Walt replied and hung up the phone.

Base Laysan, Janoesha Harbour

Four Star General David Bankole was eating dinner with his wife and daughter at The Admiral's Hall a fancy upscaled restaurant on Base Laysan. The restaurant was close to the water, the only reason why his wife and him came there was for their sixteen year old daughter Dedra, Dedra liked to watch the sailboats out on the harbour with their colorful sails. They took a table near the window so that Dedra would get to see the sailboats, the general was a pretty respectable figure on base now that Ex-General Banes was in jail. A waiter placed three menus on their table "can I get you anything to drink" he asked the Bankole family "yes I'll have a Blue Toucan in the bottle and my wife will have a martini with a lemon twist and what would you like to drink pumpkin" David asked his daughter "a Cherry-Coke please" Dedra replied "very well I'll be right back with those" the waiter said and left to get their drinks. The head chef of the restaurant came out from the kitchen and went over to where the general was sitting "it's an honor to have you and your family eating at our restaurant General, just to let you know the special today is t-bone sambar-steak seasoned in ginger, garlic, bay leaves and sumac berries served with a side order of Gungo-peas & rice" the chef informed the general and his family "that sounds good" David's wife said "just give us a few minutes" David told the chef "yes sir" the chef replied as he bowed his head in respect and left. A few minutes later the waiter came with their drinks, he put the drinks on the table "have you decided on what to eat" the waiter asked the Bankole family "give us a few minutes" David told the waiter "yes sir, enjoy your drinks I'm nearby if you need me" the waiter told David and then left. "So me and Martin was planning on going out to Hubber's Lake this weekend and I was wondering if I could borrow the jet-skies" Dedra asked her dad "I don't know, it seems a little dangerous sweetie" David replied as he looked over the menu "dad I've been jet-skying since I was eleven, I can handle myself" Dedra told her dad. David knew his daughter could handle herself, he was the first one to put her on jet-skies and she wasn't eleven she was eight, "well if your mother is okay with it I don't see why not" David told Dedra and looked over at his wife "so can I mom" Dedra asked her mother "okay but remember to leave an address and number of where you guys are staying" Dedra's mother told her "I will I promise, you guys are the best parents in the world" Dedra said to her parents excited to be given the okay. David's cell-phone started vibrating in the holder he had clipped onto his belt, he took it out and looked at the call-display, it was Walt Buyer so he answered it "oh honey you promised no work this evening" his wife said to him as he got up from around the table to take the call "it's an important call love" he told his wife as he left for the washroom to take the call "what should I tell the waiter when he comes back" his wife asked him "order me the steak" he told her. "Hello General David Bankole speaking" David answered as he went into the washroom "hi David it's Walt" Walt told him "yes Walt how is everything" David asked him "everything is well David just pulling up my driveway right now, finishing off another long day at the office, how bout you" Walt asked the general "just enjoying a nice dinner with my family but you didn't call me to shoot the breeze" David replied "no I didn't, there has been some recent developments into the investigation in the shooting of Jason Umaumbaeya, through these developments the president and I have decided on signing off on an extraction" Walt informed David "I need to know what or who my men are extracting" David told Walt "you'll be briefed tomorrow in the President's Chambers, I also need you to know the team you put together for this extraction will be put on standby until further instructed, is that clear General" Walt told him "it is sir" David complied, Walt hung up the phone on his end.

THE EXTRACTION

Base Laysan, Janoesha Harbour

The next day after he was briefed by Walt Buyer at the Orange Gate General Bankole took a military humvee back to Base Laysan where he put together a five man tactical unit for the extraction. Making up the tactical unit is Sergeant Dennis Moore their Sniper, Corporal Roy Overmill Demolition Specialist, First Sergeant Hanson Abioye & Master Sergeant Dean Chamapiwa Close Quarters Combat, heading the team would be Sergeant Major Ken Powell, he would be the one to pick up the package. The five men were sitting in a hangar waiting for their ride to Africa to fuel up, one of the men had a hand-radio tuned into 95 Kingfisher Jazz Fm a popular radio station in Alan's Landing, he put the radio on the table they were sitting around, soft Caribbean jazz music echoed throughout the hangar and out into the open air "so I heard this is blow-back from two years ago" Hanson said to his team mates "yeah they sure hold a grudge" Dennis replied as he wiped down the silencer for his sniper-rifle. Ken took a sandwich out of his gear and started eating it "what's this all about Major" Dean asked Ken "all I know is that two of our citizens are being held captive in Bethanien, Namibia, we're waiting here to be briefed on the extraction by General Bankole" Ken replied "who's holding them" Roy asked "I'm sure the general will let you know when he arrives" Ken told him and finished eating his sandwich. Ten minutes later the men watched in the hangar as a Antonov An-70 transport-plane landed on the air-strip in front of the hangar, the plane stopped in front of the hangar and its doors opened up downwards an were now steps leading to the ground. General Bankole came down the steps of the plane, he had a map rolled up under his left arm, he got to the ground and headed over to where the men were sitting, Hanson turned off his radio. The men stood up and saluted General Bankole as he came into the hangar "at ease soldiers" the general told his men. General Bankole took out the map from under his arm and spread it out on the table "okay yesterday a Cessna was stopped at Shearwater Run by the ISD, the pilot was brought into customs and questioned by the JBI, on the plane they found a bag full of stun-grenades a whole lot of foreign currency and a passport for Taitung, Taiwan, the pilot said that he was hired by a organization named The Farm to fly the plane here, the pilot and his family are Janoesians, they have his wife and daughter captive at a ranch in Bethanien, Namibia" General Bankole briefed his men as he pointed to the map. The map was a bird's-eye-view of the ranch and the areas around it, the men were looking at the map to see if there was any trails or back-roads leading to the ranch "your job men are to extract the two packages, mother and daughter and to collect or obtain any information pertinent in linking The Farm to the assassination of Jason Umaumbaeya" General Bankole said and finished his briefing "what about this wall around the ranch" Dean pointed out to General Bankole "nothing a little Semtex can't take care of" Roy interjected "that might not be a smart thing to do, we might want to look at a stealth approach" Ken told Roy. General Bankole saluted his men "you are in good hand with Sergeant Major Powell, I have faith in you and Janoesha Harbour has faith in you, your plane is ready to be boarded, I'll be keeping watch from the Orange Gate" the general told his men as he headed to an awaiting Humvee to take him back to the Orange Gate. Ken rolled up the map and kept it on him "okay men time to load up" Ken told his men, the men grabbed their gear and headed to the plane "this shouldn't take that long, I gotta get back to my sweet Mary" Hanson asked Dean on the way to the plane "sure don't worry you'll get back in time, if we don't have to deal with helicopters" Dean replied jokingly giving Hanson something to think about. The men walked up into the transport-plane, its doors closed as the last man entered in, inside the plane was quite spacious it seated fourteen men seven on one side and seven on the other. The men were sitting around a large steel chest that they used as a table, it would take the plane a hour and a half to get to Namibia, Ken rolled open the map on the chest so they can take a look at it again "looks like there's mountains surrounding the north and east of the ranch" Dean said to Ken "maybe we could do an air-drop somewhere in those mountains" Hanson suggested "that's a great idea" Ken said "our parachutes are made of see-through material so we won't be spotted from afar" he added. They studied the map a little more "we can make the drop right around here where it looks more surfaced" Ken said as he pointed to a mountainous spot on the map "what about wild animals" Roy asked "don't be a pussy, that's what your AR-15 is for" Hanson told him "it doesn't do any good if we're trying to keep silent" Roy said "he's right so no gun-fire before we breach the wall, Dennis will be stationed somewhere in the mountains with his rifle" Ken told his men, Dennis's rifle was a Barrett M95 sniper-rifle with silencer. Ken was looking at the wall around the ranch "Roy do you have any silent explosives" Ken asked Roy "I have Dexpan a non-explosive agent, drill a hole in the wall put some in the hole and problem solved, it makes no noise" Roy replied "okay men we know what we got to do so lets get our game-face on" Ken told his men, the men strapped on their parachutes "twenty minutes to the drop" Ken told the men. Twenty minutes later the plane was over the mountains of Bethanien, The Farm was just outside the town of Bethanien surrounded by mountains on its own dessert oasis, the belly-hatch of the plane opened up in the floor towards the front of the plane, the outside air rushed in and did its cycle and rushed out "okay men it's go time" Ken told his team and jumped out the open belly-hatch, one at a time the men followed behind him. They all counted to fifteen and pulled their chutes, they landed about ten feet away from their mark. When each man got both feet on the ground they released their parachutes and took out their compound cross-bows for any lurking wildlife. Dennis looked for a vantage point between two large rocks, the other men carefully headed towards the ranch with their cross-bows drawn, they walked along the dusty and hot dessert in a v formation carefully looking for any insurgents, suddenly a female lion came out from behind a rock and bolted towards Roy, Hanson saw the lioness and put two arrows from his cross-bow in her head, the lioness tumbled over in the sand dead, stopped in her tracks. Other lions started to make their appearance, coming out from behind boulders and dry bushes, the men started shooting and killing them as they came towards them. The men were now running as they killed off the remaining lions, they weren't too far from the wall when a gazelle nearly sprinted by Dean and Hanson, trying to deek between the two men, an attempt to getaway from an already dead lion, Dean didn't realize what it was and took out his machete and cut off its head with one swoop, the gazelle's headless body tumbled over and rolled at lease fifteen feet on the ground before resting up against a boulder. When they got to the wall Roy took out of his gear a small tub of already mixed Dexpan "Roy you're up" Ken told him, Roy also took out a battery operated drill and drilled four holes into the wall, the holes were twenty inches apart from each other in a circular formation, he then packed Dexpan in each hole and told everyone to stand back. Thirty seconds later the stone crumbled to pebbles opening up a hole big enough for a man to fit through "okay men the door has been opened for us, lets enter in" Ken said as he checked in the hole if they've been spotted before he went in, the men followed behind him. As the last man Dean came through the hole in the wall onto the ranch's grounds he was shot in the shoulder that spun him around and up against the wall, Hanson saw his comrade get shot and started shooting in the direction the shot came from "DEAN, you okay" Hanson asked his wounded teammate as he continued shooting but got no response. Ken just realized what just happened and saw that the shot came from a watch-tower set up beside the ranch, there is always a guard on watch there armed with a rifle "the shot came from that watch-tower" Ken told his men pointing at the tower as he continued shooting at it. A loud alert-siren went off at the ranch warning them of intruders "take cover men I think we're about to meet the welcoming committee" Ken told his men as he hid behind a thick palm-bush, Hanson grabbed Dean and they went and sat behind a large stone monument while Roy hid behind a large Sabal palm-tree. A group of twenty rebel soldiers rushed out of the ranch and stood out front with their machine-guns drawn, behind them stood in army-green fatigue and shiny black-leather boots with numerous metals pinned on his chest was Colonel Martez Jimenez, he ran and managed the ranch "YOU HAVE NOWHERE TO GO, YOU MIGHT AS WELL GIVE YOURSELVES UP" he called out to who ever blew a hole into his wall. All of a sudden two out of the twenty rebel soldiers took a couple unheard shots to the head and collapse to the ground, that caused the Colonel to head back into the ranch and the rest of the soldiers to start shooting at anything that moved. Roy still hiding behind a tree took two grenades that were hooked on his chest, pulled their pins and tossed them over to where the rebel-soldiers were, the grenades went off blowing apart three rebel-soldiers causing their body parts to propel at lease thirty feet away from the torso. The remaining rebel-soldiers split up as they continued shooting, Hanson saw a rebel-soldier coming his way "wait here pal" Hanson told Dean as he put Dean's left hand on his wounded shoulder "hold it there" he told Dean and then got ready to bull-rush the rebel-soldier, Hanson pulled his bowie-knife out of the sheath he had clipped to his belt around his waist, he waited as the rebel-soldier came closer to the stone monument, when he saw that the soldier was next to the monument he snuck up behind him and slit his throat from ear to ear, the rebel-soldier fell to his knees choking on his own blood until he fell over dead. Two more rebel-soldiers died by a bullet fired from Dennis's sniper, Ken fired his AR-15 from behind the bush killing two soldiers, Roy had a bazooka that he aimed at the watch-tower from behind the tree, he fired it, it blow up the whole watch-tower along with the guard. Hanson went back behind the monument to give aid to Dean who was sweating heavily and about to pass out from lost of blood, Hanson took a Med-Kit out of his gear and gave Dean an injection that will help keep the wound clean of infection while he bandaged up Dean's shoulder "don't worry buddy you'll be as good as new" he assured Dean. Just then the side of Dean's head sprayed out in a red-mist filled with pieces of brain and skull "NO!!" Hanson screamed as he watched his friend's body fall over dead on the ground, Hanson stood up and started firing his AR-15 (avenging Dean's death) killing three rebel-soldiers.

Spirit's Cove, Janoesha Harbour

At Shearwater Run the JBI had taken JT and his co-pilot to a holding-cell in Alan's Landing. Gary Adcliff and his men were planning a sting at the entrance to the Avis car-rental building, across the street in front of the building Gary had an agent dressed in grey-overalls and a grey-baseball-cap sitting in a blue garbage-truck with the company name Harbour Garbage & Disposal in bold-white letters on the side of it and he had a lady agent at the front desk of the Avis car-rental posing as an employee. They were waiting to see if the person the packages they got off the Cessna would come by and try to retrieve them, Gary received a tip from the co-pilot saying that they were going to wait twenty-four hours before picking up their packages so that's why he's doing the sting today. Right now it was just a waiting game, Gary was connected to everyone by CB-radio, 'JT said they would be driving an Avis rental-van' Gary thought to himself as he looked out the window of the second floor surveillance-office of the Avis Car-Rental building, the surveillance-office looked over the outdoor lobby of the building. The sting took them from 10:00 in the morning to 4:10 in the afternoon when a Avis van stopped behind the garbage-truck, someone quickly got out of the passenger-side holding a hand-gun and rolled into the nearby bushes, this took less than four seconds to do, no one really noticed when it happened. The van continued on and turned into the Avis building, the van parked in front of the entrance, no one came out of the van it was just sitting there. The young agent posing as a garbage-truck driver sat in the garbage-truck looking over at the van wondering why it was just sitting there "everyone keep your position" he heard Gary say over the CB-radio mounted on the dashboard, just then he felt the muzzle of a gun pressed up against his temple, a shot was fired and the side of the agent's head splashed out as the bullet shattered the driver's side window, his body slumped over in the truck dead, one of the men in the Avis van manage to sneak into the garbage-truck and kill the agent. The Avis van that was parked in front of the entrance, its side door opened up and a man came out holding a Minigun, he started firing it at the front of the building, bullets shattered the building's windows and tore large holes through the wooden front doors. Everyone inside took cover as the hail of bullets destroyed the front desk area, the automatic gunfire went on for a good five minutes until the man with the Minigun stopped and went back in the van, closing the door behind him, the Avis van backed out of the parking lot and its side door opened again, the guy that just killed the young man in the garbage-truck jumped into the van and closed the door the van sped off down the street. At this time Gary was now out front with his gun drawn shooting at the van as it sped away, a dark metallic-grey Jeep Wrangler filled with ISD agents came out from behind the Avis Car-Rental building and gave chase. Gary went over to where the garbage-truck was parked, he looked up into the truck's cab and found one of his agents slumped over in the seat dead from a gun shot to the head "fuck!" Gary said to himself 'how did they find out about the sting' he thought.

Bethanien, Namibia

The remaining rebel-soldiers retreated back into the ranch when they saw their numbers going down. Ken saw that Hanson was paying homage to Dean "he's dead lets go" Ken told Hanson, Hanson kissed Dean's body on the forehead "take care buddy" he told Dean and then went with Ken and Roy. The men were planning on entering into the ranch but Ken always anticipated surprises, Roy put some Semtex around the ranch's front door knob, attached to it was a wired charge. With one press of a button Roy blew the front door open and off its hinges, Ken rolled two grenades on the floor and into the ranch, when the grenades blew the men entered into the ranch. The ranch was actually a mansion with many rooms, it also had a basement and a second floor, the men split up and strategically searched the rooms on the main floor with their guns drawn. Ken took the dining room and kitchen, Hanson took the living room and study and Roy took the guest bedroom and garage, Hanson was about to go in the study when he spotted a rebel-soldier through a mirror hanging on the wall in the study, the soldier was hiding behind the door so Hanson started shooting at the wall the rebel-soldier was standing next to, bullets from Hanson's AR-15 riddled the soldier's body and the rebel-soldier fell down dead. Hearing the shooting a rebel-soldier came out of a closet in the hallway he was hiding in and was about to shoot Hanson in the back when Ken threw a Bowie-knife into the back of his head, the rebel-soldier fell to the ground like a tree that has just been chopped down "thank you" Hanson said to Ken and they both went to find Roy.

Roy was heading to the garage when he noticed just before getting there that there was a small room to the right of the door leading into the garage, this small room door was close and Roy had no idea what or who was on the other side of it. Roy took out of his gear an explosive that looked like a hockey-puck, he slid the explosive on the floor to the door of the small room, the explosive stopped right next to the door and went off causing the door to bow inward and blow open, the rebel-soldier that was in there started shooting but the door knocked him backwards and up against a washing-machine, the rebel-soldier went to raise his gun and shoot Roy but before that could happen Roy unloaded on him with his AR-15 nearly decapitating the rebel-soldier. Hanson and Ken met up with Roy in the main floor hallway "did you check the garage" Hanson asked Roy "yeah no one in there" Roy replied "where do you think their holding them" Hanson asked Ken referring to the woman and child their there to rescue "I'm not sure but we are going to check this whole place" Ken told him. They headed down to the basement, the basement was divided up into four rooms, the first room they came upon they heard voices inside, the door was slightly open, Roy rolled a smoke-bomb canister in the room, as soon as it went off the men rushed in the room and shot and killed the three rebel-soldiers that were inside. Ken saw that there was three security monitors setup in the room, two showed the ranches property and the surrounding dessert and the other showed upstairs where they were holding the woman and child "now we know where they are" Ken said to his men. The men looked at the monitor, it showed a large round loft-like room that was above the second floor office, a brass spiral banister lead up there from the office, in the room is a brass frame water-bed with a alpaca-fur comforter over it at the far side of the room, there's a desk made of Cherry-wood facing the banister, sitting behind it is Colonel Jimenez smoking a Cuban cigar, on the bed sits a young woman, cuddled up next to her holding a teddy-bear in her left hand and holding her lady's hand with her right was a little girl, there were four rebel-soldiers standing guard around them. Ken could see on the monitor that the woman and child were very scared "that's the package men" Ken reminded his men as he pointed at the woman and child on the monitor. They headed up to the loft "keep it tight men, we don't know what to expect" Ken said as him and his men carefully and in S.W.A.T formation made their way upstairs, they took a few minutes to clear the second floor of any rebel-soldier. Mapping it out perfectly Hanson stood in the small washroom to the second floor office and shot up through the ceiling with his AR-15 killing two rebel-soldiers and causing a diversion for Ken and Roy to rush up the banister, Ken killed the remaining two rebel-soldiers and Roy put one between the eyes of Colonel Jimenez with his Beretta 92 before the Colonel could pull his gun and shoot Ken. "Check the desk" Ken told Roy as he went over to the woman and child "are you hurt" Ken asked the woman and child while he knelt down in front of them checking them for any cuts and bruises "we're okay" the young lady replied "can you walk" Ken asked her "yes I can walk" the lady replied. Ken helped the lady to her feet and the little girl climbed up on his back, they made their way down to the main floor "did you find anything" Ken asked Roy as they headed downstairs "some papers, looks like business transactions from a bank in Arion, Belgium" Roy told him, they met up with Hanson when they got to the second floor "what's the name of the company that sent the funds" Ken asked Roy "it shows that a De Smet Exploration & Games deposited a million British-pounds three different times into an account The Farm has here in Windhoek" Roy replied. "You guys okay" Hanson asked Ken and Roy "we're fine" Ken replied as they headed down to the main floor "the colonel reports in to someone every hour, more soldiers will be coming if they don't get his report" the young lady informed Ken as they got to the main floor hallway "what's your name mam" Ken asked her "Rochelle" she replied "Rochelle no need to worry we have a plane out in the mountains that will fly you and your daughter to safety" Ken assured her. When they got to the front door Hanson and Roy went up front to protect the package, they came out front with their guns drawn "looks clear Major" Hanson told Ken, Ken came outside with Rochelle and her daughter, they made their way to the hole in the wall. "Remember men when we get outside the wall there may be more wild animals to deal with" Ken told his men. At the hole in the wall Roy tossed a couple stun-grenades through the hole and then a regular grenade, he waited for them to go off, after the last one went off he went through the hole first with his Beretta 92 out ready to shoot any attacking animal. "Okay lets go" Ken said to Rochelle and her daughter, he helped them through the hole and followed behind them, Hanson was the last one through the hole "when's the last time the colonel made a report" Hanson asked Rochelle as he came through the hole "about forty minutes ago" Rochelle replied "so we have twenty minutes to make a clean getaway" Hanson said to her. They started hiking through the hot dessert back towards the mountains where Dennis was "Gunny this is Major we're heading back to the pick-up right now copy" Ken reported to Dennis on his walkie-talkie but got no response "what do you think Major" Roy asked Ken concerned about Dennis "he could be trying to stay discreet from animals" Ken replied. Hanson riddled a tiger jogging towards them with bullets from his AR-15, the large cat fell over on its side dead. A zebra sprinted by them looking like it was running from something, the men went into a S.W.A.T formation around the packages as they kept walking towards the mountains "don't worry we won't let anything happen to you" Ken told Rochelle and her daughter. Just then to the right of them Hanson saw four hyenas running towards them about fifty feet away, Hanson started shooting the dog-like animals, he killed two of them but the other two fanned out in opposite directions "look alive they might come back" Ken told his men "don't worry they'll be more" Hanson said sarcastically. They weren't too far from the mountains now just over twenty yards away, one of the two hyenas that left came back and tried to sneak up behind Roy but Roy saw it coming and pulled out his machete chopping off its head, the headless body of the spotted Carnivora fell over on its side as blood gushed out of its severed neck, Roy put his machete back in its sheath. The men were now on an inclined path leading into the mountains, Ken lifted up Rochelle's daughter and carried her on his back "Hanson find Dennis he should be close by" Ken told Hanson "I'll radio in for pick up" Ken continued "yes sir"

Hanson said and left. Hanson went north along a rugged surface of rock and quartz to a dirt trail leading to a higher escarpment of rock, he didn't see anything as he walked along the trail, when he got to where the escarpment was he looked up and spotted the butt-end of a rifle. Hanson climbed up the escarpment to see if it was Dennis "GUNNY IS THAT YOU" he called out as he climbed up to the surface but got no answer. When Hanson got to the surfaced top he saw a sniper-rifle laying halfway off the escarpment not too far from it was a dead body in a semi-dried pool of blood under a tan colored ghillie-suit, the body was missing its head and right hand, Hanson knew it was Dennis because of the uniform with the Janoesian flag sewn on the right should "goodbye friend" he said as he stared at the body. Hanson stooped down over the body and with his bowie-knife cut the flag from off the should and put it in his breast-pocket along with Dennis's dog-tags, he went over to where the rifle was laying and pick it up, he put it in with his gear and carried on his way back down the escarpment. After radioing in for pick up Ken, Roy and the packages were camped out under a slab of weather-polished slate that toppled over onto a large boulder "I set in our coordinates, they should be here in a few minutes" Ken assured the others "Major I put up a line of trip-wire with shock-charge in the outside perimeters so we should be safe here" Roy informed Ken "thank you Corporal" Ken told him. Suddenly they heard a high-pitch whistle in the distance "do you hear that" Roy asked Ken, Ken looked at him and nodded his head "yeah I hear it, what is it" Rochelle asked Roy looking concerned. The whistling stopped for a few minutes and started up again, this time it sound much closer "it's close by" Rochelle said, Roy had a hunch he whistled back and the whistling stopped an went into a bird-call "it's Hanson he's near by" Roy told them. They heard the engines of the Antonov An-70 transport-plane hovering over them "okay everybody time to go" Ken said and brought Rochelle and her daughter out from under the rock, two rope-ladders were thrown down from the transport-plane, Rochelle climbed up one and Ken the other with Rochelle's daughter on his back. Hanson met up with Roy waiting for his turn to climb up and that came soon enough along with Hanson's turn so they both climbed up into the plane together "where's Dennis" Ken asked Hanson as he sat down in the plane with Roy "sorry Major he didn't make it" Hanson replied "but I did get his dog-tags and country-crest" he told Ken "do have his weapon" Ken asked Hanson "yeah I grabbed that to, it's in my pack" Hanson replied "then you did good soldier" Ken informed him. "What happened" Roy asked Hanson curious "I don't know I just found his body, his head and right hand were missing so I did what any other soldier would do and left" Hanson told him. The plane was now leaving Namibian air-space and flying northwest over the Atlantic "thank you for coming for us" Rochelle told the three soldiers "is my husband safe" she asked the soldiers "yes he's in custody on Janoesha Harbour" Ken assured her, Rochelle gave out a sy and smile of relief, her daughter hugged her and Rochelle kissed her on her head "thank you" she said to Ken, Ken gave her a smile and nodded his head in service. The plane was now flying over Guinea, far up in the clouds, hard for someone or signal to spot "so you're from Brookshore" Roy asked Rochelle "yes most of my life" Rochelle replied "yeah I use to play college-ball there back in the day, I always liked the nightlife there" Roy told Rochelle "it is a busy city" she said smiling to herself in reminiscence "must be a busy place for a wildlife photographer" Hanson asked interceding, Rochelle felt a tone of interrogation in Hanson's voice "it can be at times" she replied staunchly. Hanson smiled at Rochelle and then started eating an energy-bar he found in his pack. The plane was now entering Janoesian air-space, it flew halfway over Janoesha Harbour and hovered over Alan's Landing, the plane landed on a large helipad near the garden behind the Orange Gate. The doors to the Antonov An-70 opened up and the men exited the plane with Rochelle and her daughter, they were greeted by Walt Buyer and General Bankole and two Orange Gate Security Agents "well done Major" General Bankole said to Ken after they saluted each other and he shook his hand. Walt looked at Rochelle and her daughter "hi I'm Defense Minister Walt Buyer, mam I need a few moments of your time" he said to Rochelle "I know who you are, I've seen you on TV, where's my husband" Rochelle asked Walt "he's safe, he's in a holding-cell here in Alan's Landing" Walt replied "after a few questions we can take you to him" Walt told her, she agreed. Rochelle and her daughter went with Walt and the two Security Agents to Walt's office where they met up with the President, Rochelle and her daughter sat in two chairs in front of Walt's desk, the President sat to the left of them in another chair and Walt sat on the edge of his desk in front of Rochelle, the two Security Agents were standing guard outside the door "what's your name mam" Walt asked Rochelle "Rochelle Haddler"

Rochelle replied "and your daughter" Walt asked "Tiana" Rochelle replied. Walt crossed his arms over his chest "I think you know how serious this is" Walt said to Rochelle and then waited for a physical or emotional reply but all Rochelle did was look at him "your husband is facing smuggling charges" Walt told her "he's innocent" Rochelle said to Walt "he was cot smuggling weapons and money into the country" Walt informed her "that money is from a group of Belgium businessmen, I saw them load it on the plane" Rochelle told Walt "you were there when they loaded the plane" Walt asked her "not exactly, I was upstairs in the ranch but I could see everything from the window" Rochelle replied "were the businessmen in the ranch" Walt inquired "yeah for about a half an hour and then a helicopter came for them" Rochelle answered. Walt could tell that so far Rochelle was telling the truth so he continued questioning her "what were they doing in the ranch" Walt asked her "they were speaking with Colonel Jimenez, when we met him he said his name was Ronald, that bastard!" Rochelle replied referring to Colonel Jimenez "what were they talking about" Walt inquired "never got the whole conversation the parts a got were that they are part of a hunting club and that they're next hunt will be on Janoesha Harbour and after that Taiwan, I also heard them say to the colonel that they gave The Farm eleven million Euros to get rid of a problem, I don't know what that means" Rochelle informed Walt. Walt looked at President Myers and then back at Rochelle "okay I guess that's enough for now, you can leave, security will escort you to a sitting room until someone can take you to see your husband" Walt informed her, Rochelle and Tiana left the room and went with the two Security Agents. "So what do you think" President Myers asked Walt "I think it's all adding up" Walt replied "yep I think you're right" the president agreed "so there is a contract, possibly a hit-list" Walt said "if this thing is international I'm going to have to call Alex Williams at The Branch" President Myers told Walt.

Alex Williams is the Director Of The (ACIB) Albatross Crest International Intelligence Branch, the citizens of Janoesha Harbour call them ACIB, the government calls them The Branch. They are similar to the American CIA, the ACIB building is located in downtown Alan's Landing at 37 Savannah Court, down the street from the Orange Gate, the Orange Gate is located at 35 Savannah Court.

Walt looked at President Myers "yes you're right sir, we're going to need some intelligence on this for more information" Walt told him "I just told my secretary to give Alex a call" the president informed Walt.

3

IN THE CIRCLE OF INTELLIGENCE

Alan's Landing, Janoesha Harbour

The next day in Alan's Landing the weather was foggy and sunny at the same time, the sun shun through the trees making the fog look like smoke coming off their leaves. Bailey Gcobani showed up at the Orange Gate by black Lincoln Limousine, Bailey Gcobani is a Field-Agent of the third rank for the ACIB, a third rank agent is the highest rank you can be at the Branch working out in the field, field-agents report to their Great Tross, a Great Tross commands a team of agents. The limo parked at the front door of the Orange Gate, its back door opened and Bailey came out, he was wearing a dark-grey classic fit two piece suit with a black-tie with white polka-dots, on his feet he had on a comfortable pair of black elk-skin oxfords. Bailey was greeted by the president's secretary "hello Mr. Gcobani welcome to the Orange Gate" she said as she shook his hand, Bailey is a very handsome young man and has a charm about him that the ladies can't get enough of but the president's secretary was aware of this and she stood her ground well "and what's your name" Bailey asked her as he enjoyed her lady-like appearance "Joyce, follow me" she told him so he followed her into the Orange Gate. She took him down a large hallway made of varnished mahogany wood and carpeted with red-carpet, hanging on the walls in the hallway were framed pictures of past presidents, two Janoesian flags hung on their posts on both sides of a large wooden door at the end of the hallway. They came to the door to the president's office, Joyce opened the door "Mr. Gcobani is here sir" she informed President Myers as Bailey entered in the room "thank you Joyce" the president said to her, Joyce left the room closing the door behind her. Walt Buyer was also in the president's office sitting in a chair, "how are you agent" President Myers asked Bailey "you know, same old" Bailey replied nonchalantly "we have a problem agent" the president told him "yeah I know I was breifed by Alex" Bailey informed the president as he took a seat in the chair beside Walt "I believe we share the same problem" Bailey told the president "how so" Walt asked intrigued "the Branch bugged an apartment in Brussels, Belgium owned by Emile Peeters a wealthy aristocrat, we've been following him and listening to his conversations for the past two years" Bailey informed the president and Walt. "What did you find out" Walt asked Bailey "well most of it is classified but what I can tell you is that Emile Peeters is the Farm's European connection, we've traced a number of wired-transfers to a bank in Bayamo, Cuba coming from Arion, Belgium where Peeters owns a house" Bailey informed them "what about the assassination of Jason Umaumbaeya" President Myers asked Bailey "I'm sorry to hear about that and we will find who pulled the trigger but if this is the Farm's doing they don't do much without the approval of Emile Peeters, if you believe it's a contracted hit then there's a very good chance that Peeters put up the money to make it happen" Bailey told the president. Walt sat up straight in his chair "actually we believe it's a hit-list" Walt told Bailey "I believe that" Bailey agreed "what do you mean" Walt asked him "what happened here over two years ago really put a ripple in Emile Peeters sail, he's not one to forget, those involved should be concerned" Bailey replied "are you saying the president's life is in danger" Walt asked Bailey with a concerned look on his face "if there is a hit-list we should anticipate that your name's on it Mr. President and from now on have tight security around you" Bailey replied as he looked at President Myers. Walt looked at President Myers then back at Bailey "I was recently told about a De Smet Exploration & Games located in Arion, Belgium, are they related to Emile Peeters" Walt asked Bailey "yes Emile Peeters owns that company, they also recruit hunters from The Farm" Bailey replied "is the Branch close to breaking up his operation" Walt inquired "it's going to take time, his family is connected to German Royalty but we're getting close" Bailey told him "is there any other news agent" President Myers asked Bailey "are you in contact with a Captain Moses Uatobuu because you should anticipate that he's also in danger" Bailey told them.

Tamerra, Janoesha Harbour

Jeff was in his SUV driving on Route 51 in downtown Tamerra, the heavy security watch by the ISD and JBI in the downtown core was now just a few ISD agents patrolling the streets. Jeff parked the SUV near the corner of Route 51 and 24 in an alley behind a bakery, he got out of the vehicle and grabbed his briefcase off the backseat and closed the door, he climbed up a fire-escape to the roof of the bakery and then went up another fire-escape leading to the roof of a higher adjacent building. Jeff liked the vantage point he had for now, he laid there on the roof in his ghillie-suit looking through the scope of his rifle at all the insignificant people walking on the sidewalk below 'he could peg them all off like ducks in a shooting gallery' he thought but right now he was looking for one special duck (Moses Uatobuu), he knows he comes into town this time of the day so he laid there waiting. Forty minutes later while he was looking through the scope and eating an energy-bar he spotted Moses in a Ford F-150 driving along Route 25 just about to cross over Route 53 "too bad you're alone" Jeff said to himself as he watch the F-150 through the scope of his rifle. He was aiming at one of the back tires, as soon as the tire came into the view of his scope he fired a unheard shot that flattened the tire causing the hub-cap to roll off onto the sidewalk almost killing a pedestrian, Jeff smiled to himself as he cleared the chamber of his rifle.

Moses came into town to pick up some meat from the deli, some sausages and Sambar-steaks, and also do some running around for Stacey, she had giving him a long list of places to go and things to buy and that's what he was doing, he would do her list before he went to the deli. Moses turned off Route 52 onto Route 25 that lead to Opal Gallery Mall where he had to pick some stuff up, just before getting to Route 53 his right back tire exploded and his pickup started swerving in the road before crashing into a light-post "what the fuck!" Moses said to himself as he took off his seat-belt and opened the door, just as Moses got out of the vehicle two more shots shattered the pickup's windshield "shit!" Moses said as he ran around to the back of the pickup and ducked down. 'Someone is shooting at him' Moses thought to himself as he shielded himself behind the pick-up "it's probably that fucker from the bistro" he said to himself. Moses saw two ISD agents running up to him, they were on patrol when they seen Moses crash into the light-post. They came up to Moses crouched down behind his pickup "are you okay sir" one of the ISD agents asked Moses but before Moses could answer him a bullet hit the agent between the eyes, the back of his head sprayed out in a red mist of pieces of skull and brain, the agent fell to the ground dead in front of Moses. The other agent started shooting towards the roof of the building in front of him (it was more like panic-fire), the agent ran and hid behind a newspaper-box on the other side of Route 25. Moses had changed into Silverback, he grabbed his sword and whip out of his pickup and started climbing up the side of a building, a shot hit him in the shoulder but all he did was growl and then leaped from the building over Route 25 onto the roof of a lower building. Silverback spotted the glint of Jeff's rifle's scope reflecting off the sun's rays, he was on the roof of the Janoesian Doctrine

Of Commerce building so Silverback cautiously and with plenty of versatility made his way there, on his way there more bullets came at him which he deflected with his sword "I'M COMING TO GET YOU" Silverback called out to Jeff as he stood on the roof of a building on the other side of Route 25 the same height as the one Jeff was on. Jeff stood up and looked at Silverback in unbelief, he pull out his Beretta M9 from its holster and started shooting at Silverback which didn't effected Silverback at all. With his sword in front of him Silverback leaped from the building he was at onto the roof of the building Jeff was, Jeff grabbed his rifle and made a run for the fire-escape and headed down to the lower adjacent building and then down to the alley where his SUV was parked. Silverback saw Jeff get into a grey SUV parked in the alley so he climbed down the back of the building into the alley, before Silverback could get to him Jeff sped off and turned onto Route 51 heading north, Silverback chased after him swinging on light-posts and running along sides of buildings at a rapid speed. Jeff looked through his rear-view mirror and saw Silverback running on Route 51 after him as various vehicles prevented from hitting the large creature. Jeff rolled down the driver's side window and started shooting at Silverback while operating the SUV with his other hand. Silverback eventually got up beside the SUV and started shoulder-checking the side of the vehicle trying to knock it off the road, Jeff was about to shoot him with his Beretta M9 when Silverback swatted it out of his hand nearly breaking Jeff's arm "FUCK!" Jeff screamed out in pain as he controlled the vehicle from spinning out of control with his healthy hand. When Jeff got to Route 23 he made a sharp right turn and headed east to Pearles, this caused Silverback to roll and crash into the display window of a clothing store because he was too heavy to turn sharp corners on a dime, It allowed Jeff to distance himself from Silverback but not for long because Silverback started up the chase once more, this time keeping a distance behind and following the SUV seeing where it leads him. Luckily for Silverback there was enough cars and trucks on Route 23 to shield him from Jeff's sight. When Jeff got to Pearles he turned left onto Route 62, he looked through his rearview mirror and spotted Silverback in the distance hiding behind the trunk of a large Sequoia-tree "looks like I'm being followed" Jeff said to himself. When Jeff got to Route 22 he made a right turn leading Silverback away from his cabin, he drove west on Route 22 until he got to Route 64 then he headed south. All this time Silverback was following him but not attacking, just perched in trees watching the SUV to see where it goes. There was a lot of trees and dense bush there, they were steps away from the Ormetha Hills, this was an advantage for Silverback, Silverback sat on a rock escarpment behind a palm-bush looking down at the SUV driving along Route 64.

Alan's Landing, Janoesha Harbour

Walt Buyer went to the Legislature Building to speak with the Attorney General Otis Bryne, they were sitting in the General's Chambers, the Legislature Building is located at 36 Savannah Court, it is where federal and regional laws are passed, the building is built of polished ivory-stone blocks, it looks similar to a slave-master's house in the American south. "General we have an issue that seemed to evolve internationally" Walt said to Otis "well I would think being Defense Minister there would be a few hurdles you would have to leap over" the Attorney General replied "yes you're right, I guess what I'm looking for is a resolution to a covert attack" Walt said to Otis "what are we talking about Walt" Otis asked Walt concerned about what the Defense Minister was talking about "I was just informed by the Branch that money from a bank in Belgium is being wired every month to a bank in Bayamo, Cuba to fund an illegal hunting expedition right here on Janoesha Harbour, most likely in the Black Forest" Walt informed the Attorney General. Otis crossed his arms over his chest and shook his head in disbelief "that's preposterous, nothing like that is happening" he told Walt "it's all being organized by an Emile Peeters a wealthy Aristocrat from Belgium" Walt told Otis "I know who Emile Peeters is and he's far from being an international villain, he's a philanthropist and businessman in Belgium, he just finished building a child's care hospital in Brussels" Otis said to Walt "I'm thinking of planning a covert attack on Belgium" Walt told Otis "under what grounds" Otis asked him "under the grounds I just finished telling you" Walt replied "Walt that would be a breach of international justice" the Attorney General informed him "Otis he's funding a hunt on Janoesha Harbour" Walt reminded Otis in a stern voice "that's enough Admiral" Otis told Walt as the tone of his voice rose a level "how bout a covert attack on Cuba" Walt asked him "well I guess if it was only to gather Intel we could get around the legalities" Otis replied "when were you planning this for" Otis asked Walt "a week from now" Walt replied "okay I'll sign off on it but only to collect Intel" Otis told him.

The next day in downtown Alan's Landing at Jordan Square a military award ceremony was happening for the soldiers that rescued the two Janoesian Citizens from their captor in Namibia. This time the Square was heavily guarded by Military Police and ACIB Agents watching the outer perimeter of the Square, some of them were perched up on roofs of buildings surrounding the Square. President Myers was there with General Bankole, standing on the other side of the president was Bailey Gcobani, Walt Buyer was also there with his wife Elaine, she's a Major General in the military. Medals were being awarded to Sergeant Major Ken Powell, First Sergeant Hanson Abioye and Corporal Roy Overmill, the three soldiers stood on a stage overlooking a crowd of military service-men and women plus curious on-lookers gathering in off the streets. The three soldiers were about to receive the Janoesian Medallion which in the military is known as The Janoesian Medal of Bravery & Justice, the medal was on a shiny-blue lanyard with a black-stripe down the middle of it, President Myers hung the medals around the soldiers necks and shook their hand. President Myers said a speech thanking the soldiers for their bravery. After President Myers finished his speech and left, General Bankole stepped up on the stage, he shook his soldiers hands and saluted them. General Bankole had come up on stage to give each soldier an extra stripe on their uniform, they were being ranked-up, Ken Powell became a Command Sergeant Major, Hanson Abioye a Sergeant Major and Roy Overmill a Sergeant, the three soldiers smiled, raised their right arm and waved to the crowd as the multitude of people cheered and clapped for them, they exited the stage behind General Bankole. After the ceremony there was a buffet set up in the Square under a large blue canope, there was also a live brass jazz-band playing at the other end of the Square, it was now social-hour, a time to mingle. Most of the servicemen were lined up along the buffet-tables getting there plates of food, the buffet also came with a wide selection of cold drinks including wine-coolers, most of the servicewomen are a fan of wine-coolers. Elaine Buyer was sitting around a table that was set up in the Square enjoying a Passion-fruit wine-cooler while she waited for her husband to get her something to eat from the buffet. Walt came to the table his wife was sitting at with two plates of food in his hands, he put down a plate on the table in front of Elaine "this is for you my love" he said to her and then sat down next to her while placing his plate of food on the table in front of him, there was silver-wear, napkins and a clear glass-jug of water already set up on the table, there was at lease forty tables set up in the Square, each table has a brown wicker-basket filled with fresh-fruits in the center of it. Walt was halfway through his meal when President Myers came to his table "good to see you Walt" the president said to him as he approached his table, Walt smiled at Sterling "hi sir" Walt replied, the president stood next to Walt "good day mam" President Myers said to Elaine as he bowed his head in respect "nice seeing you again" he told her, Elaine gave him a smile and took a drink of her wine-cooler. "I heard you had a little visit with the Attorney General yesterday" President Myers said to Walt as he turned to face him, Walt looked at his wife "can you get me a beer hon" he asked Elaine, Elaine knew what he meant by that 'he wants a little private time to speak with the president' she thought to herself "sure what would you like love" Elaine replied and got up from around the table "a Blue Toucan is fine" Walt told her, Elaine left and went to the buffet-table. Walt put down his knife and fork and looked up at President Myers "have a seat sir" he offered the president a chair, President Myers took a seat next to Walt "we were going over the legalities of a covert attack on Belgium" Walt told the president "what did he say" the president asked Walt "he said we can't do it, it's a breach of international justice" Walt replied "well he's right, it is" President Myers told him "he did say we can do a covert attack on Cuba only to gather Intel" Walt informed President Myers "this might workout good for us, gather enough evidence to charge them in the world's court, we can chop the head and tail off the snake, metaphorically speaking" the president told Walt "yeah maybe" Walt said as he picked up the jug of water and poured himself a glass "this time it can't be the army, we need someone to infiltrate The Farm" Walt told President Myers "how about Bailey Gcobani" President Myers asked Walt "no he's too close, we need a new face someone they won't expect" Walt told him "the only other person I can think of is Jackson Ames for The Branch" the president told Walt. Walt took a drink of his water "is he any good" Walt asked President Myers "he's sort of a Spy-Specialist for The Branch, he's thirty-four years old and single without kids, the only dedication he has is to his work" President Myers informed Walt "he would have to be in deep cover for awhile, that means limited connection with The Branch" Walt told the president "I'll speak with Alex" President Myers said to Walt.

Pearles, Janoesha Harbour

Jeff was eating lunch at a diner near Stage Park Theater, he sat at a table by the window so he would be able to see who came in off the street, after that wild-ride yesterday Jeff's not taking any chances. He sat there around the table looking at a information-sheet on his laptop, the sheet was on a Sterling Alton Myers, it said that Mr. Myers was born in Portland, Jamaica in 1959, his parents immigrated to Janoesha Harbour in 1961, Sterling grew up in the City of Brookshore where he played Regional Kelo-Ball all through high school, he graduated from the University of Janoesha Harbour in Alan's Landing in 1983 with a Masters in Constitutional Law and Political Studies, he then went on to become a Prosecuting Lawyer at Hassan & Benowitz Law Firm for twenty years before getting into politics at the age of forty-five, Sterling was elected as the President of Janoesha Harbour in 2009, there was a inset picture of President Myers on the information-sheet. Jeff looked up from the laptop's screen "where's the waitress" he said to himself as he looked around for her, couple minutes later she came over to his table "what can I get you sir" she asked him, Jeff knew what he wanted he already looked over the menu "can I get a Smoked Turkey Sandwich with Sweet-potato fries" he said to the waitress "coming right up, would you like anything to drink with that" she inquired "yes a Blue Toucan please" Jeff replied, the waitress left to get him a beer and order his lunch. Jeff turned his attention back to the information-sheet 'I think I'm going to have to give Moses Uatobuu a rest for now and go after Sterling Myers' Jeff thought to himself, he searched through the internet and saw on TJNX Net News that President Myers was making a public appearance at Hope Stadium in Alan's Landing for the kick off of the Kelo-Ball Playoffs. The waitress came back with Jeff's beer "here you go sir" she said to him as she placed the bottle of beer on the table in front of him "your meal will be ready soon" she told him and left, Jeff took a drink of his beer still staring at his laptop 'the stadium would be his chance to hit the President' Jeff thought to himself. The waitress came with Jeff's meal and placed it on the table beside his laptop, she was also holding a small metal rack of condiments which she put down next to his plate of food "thank you, this looks great" Jeff told her, the waitress smiled, she noticed that Jeff's beer was halfway done "would you like another beer sir" she asked him, Jeff looked at his beer and took a drink "sure thank you" he replied, the waitress left to get him another Blue Toucan. Jeff was still watching TJNX News on his laptop, the news said the Kelo-Ball Playoffs starts in two days at 11:00am, that's all Jeff needed to know, he would be there at the starting game. Jeff turned off his laptop, closed it and put it in his bag, he started eating his turkey sandwich, with his other hand he poured ketchup over his fries and started to occasionally eat them with a fork. After Jeff finished eating his lunch he sat at the table and drank his beer as he watched the TV mounted on the wall above the diner's front counter, it was showing the news from Alan's Landing, ANFJ News AtNoon. The news said that the Kelo-Ball Playoffs will start on August 30th, 2022 "that's in two days" Jeff said to himself, the news said that the event has been sold-out so anyone that is waiting to receive their ticket online should call their local Ticket Master for a refund. The news continued to report that earlier today there was a military award ceremony in Jordan Square, quite a few dignitaries were there amongst a crowd of people like Defense Minister Walt Buyer and the First Lady Gloria Myers with her husband President Myers. Jeff ordered another beer and kept watching the news "the president really gets around here" Jeff said to himself, the waitress overheard him when she came back to give him the beer he ordered and thought he was speaking to her "yeah he even went jet-skiing at Hubber's Lake" she told him, Jeff gave her a odd look "can I get the bill please" he asked her "coming right up" the waitress replied and left to get the bill.

Tamerra, Janoesha Harbour

Jackson Ames was sitting on the hood of his powder-blue 1965 convertible Plymouth Valiant out front of the Space Lab, he was watching the construction workers as they worked on rebuilding the Space Lab. Jackson sat there eating a six inch Steak & Cheese Sub and drinking a Red-Iguana Fountain Soda, he loved visiting the Space Lab as a kid even now as an adult he still likes it, four years ago he brought a date here and she really loved it to "don't worry they're working on you, you'll be here forever" Jackson said to himself, directing it to the Space Lab. After Jackson finished his sub he went back behind the wheel of his car, with his vanity coming into play he checked his face in the rear-view mirror, combing his eye-brows with his index-finger. His cell-phone started ringing on the dashboard, he answered it "Ames speaking" Jackson said, it was The Branch "okay I'll be there in an hour" he said and hung up the phone. Jackson started up his car and headed south on Route 50, he was going to Base Laysan, his Great Tross told him to go there and report to a Walt Buyer at the General's Quarters. Jackson was planning on painting the interior of his house in the Rockhound neighborhood later on today, 'I guess it will have to wait' he thought to himself, Jackson knew Walt Buyer from seeing him on the TV 'he's the country's Defense Minister' he thought to himself "I wonder what he wants with me" Jackson said to himself not knowing what was going on. Jackson took Route 50 until he got to Route 20, he made a right turn onto Route 20 and stayed on Route 20 until he got to Route 20 & 54 and then made a left turn on to Route 54, Jackson stayed on Route 54 all the way to the city limit. Jackson has been working for The Branch for sixteen years, they recruited him right after he finished Young Rangers, he was a former Green Caiman in the Young Rangers, only a hand-full of Rangers get the Green Caiman Badge, that's the highest achievable rank in the Young Rangers. Jackson merged onto Highway 32 from Route 54, that section of Highway 32 bridged over Route 55 for a couple kilometers. Jackson loved to look at the Atlantic from the highway, the sailboats that sat on its crystal-blue waters seemed so picturesque to him. After driving for a good fifty minutes Jackson scene the exit sign for Base Laysan, he exited off the highway onto Route 70 that went into Base Laysan, it was a nice drive along Route 70 after a couple miles it turned into a two lane freeway going through quaint neighborhoods and plush-green meadows with barns and old country-style gas stations. It didn't take Jackson that long to get to Base Laysan from the highway, Jackson stopped at the front gate of the base, an MP Officer stepped out of the booth at the front gate and came over to Jackson's car "can I help you sir" the officer asked him "I'm here to see Walt Buyer in the General's Quarters" Jackson replied as he showed the MP Officer his ACIB identification "yes sir go right ahead" the officer told him as the gate opened up. Jackson waited for the gate to open all the way before he drove onto the base, this is not Jackson's first time at Base Laysan he did his Special Weapons and Combat Training here for The Branch. For weapons Jackson carries a SIG Sauer P320 handgun, a Benchmade Adamas Folders knife and a Boot-knife, he is also very proficient in LaambWrestling and Israeli Krav Maga.

Tuesday, August 30th 2022, Alan's Landing, Janoesha Harbour

Jeff had showed up to Hope Stadium early in the day, about 3:00 in the morning, he set himself up on the roof of the stadium facing the jumbo-tron, he knew the president would be sitting in the VIP box over the stage which is right under the jumbo-tron. He laid on the roof of the stadium in his ghillie suit for hours eating his energy-bars and looking through his rifle's scope, waiting for the president to arrive. When the sun came up a long line of people accumulated at the front doors of Hope Stadium. Most of them were painted in their team's colors and chanting and singing praise for their team, the teams that were playing this morning were The Hannon Dragons vs The Umni Tross. The doors were going to open in the next thirty minutes, Jeff kept looking through his scope at the VIP box, this was going to be a clean kill for him with enough time to dispose of the evidence "make it perfect, just do the job and collect the money" Jeff said to himself as he looked through his scope and caressed his rifle's trigger with his right index-finger. After a few minutes the stadium's doors opened up and the crowd of people poured in, they went into the aisles looking for their seats. Hope Stadium is a large stadium, for sporting events it seats sixty thousand for concerts seventy-five thousand, the stadium was full for this daytime game, there was another game being played here at 5:00 in the evening today between The Brookshore Ocelots and the Sharesta Plain Ramblers. The crowd clapped and cheered as President Myers entered in the VIP box with his security, accompanying him was General Bankole and his daughter Dedra along with the First Lady Gloria Myers. President Myers waved to the crowd before he sat down next to his wife, he watched with Gloria as the teams came out on the field, the teams stood side by side looking at the Janoesian flag as it was lowered down to the field, the crowd stood up as the Janoesian National Anthem was played. Cheers, claps and whistles came from the crowd when the anthem was finish, President Myers was now on the field to flip the coin for the starting kick-off. Hope Stadium was under heavy security, the local police and a few ISD agents were helping with security, every level of the stadium had a couple security-guards on patrol with an ISD agent but not the rooftop of the stadium. Usually Hope Stadium's roof would be closed but fortunately for Jeff today was very warm on Janoesha Harbour and the roof was left open plus the blimp from ANFJ News was broadcasting from above the stadium. "He looks good on the field" Dedra said to Gloria as they stopped clapping and sat down, Gloria didn't say anything she just smiled in appreciation and agreement, "who are you cheering for Dee" General Bankole asked his daughter "I'm a Tross fan" Dedra replied but truthfully she had a crush on the goaltender for Umni Tross.

Jeff watched through the scope of his rifle as President Myers flipped the coin for the starting kick-off "calm down, slow, take your time, be patient" he said to himself. President Myers just finished flipping the coin and was now being escorted off the field by his security and a couple local police officers. The president was surround by his security and the police as they walked off the field, just then a unheard shot went off and a bullet pierced the head of the Security Officer directly behind President Myers, blood sprayed out on the president. The bullet entered in a downward angle and exited out his right cheek causing a large exit wound where his cheek and right eye was, the officer collapsed to the ground dead. The other Security Officers saw the body of their fallen comrade and rushed the president off the field, just then two more bullets killed a police officer beside the president. Security managed to get President Myers off the field and down into underground parking where his limo was. In the stadium the teams had exited the field and the crowd was told to stay in their seats and to make sure that friends and family are all accounted for, the stadium officials played music videos on the jumbo-tron to keep the crowd of people entertained. Jeff packed up his rifle and made his way off the roof, he was upset with himself, he missed three times in killing Sterling Myers "I had him in my sight and I fucking! missed" he said to himself. Jeff shimmied down a large cable that was hanging from the roof onto a small fire-escape, the door was open to the fire-escape and there was a security-guard just inside the open doorway, before Jeff landed on the fire-escape he pulled out his handgun and shot the guard in the head killing him instantly. An ISD agent heard the shot and ran to see what was going on, Jeff made his way down to the next level where he went out a fire-exit to another fire-escape, took the fire-escape down to the street-level. Before Jeff got to the ground he could see that an ISD agent was standing under the ladder of the fire-escape, the agent just finished answering a call about a shooting at the stadium and to look out for any suspicious person or activity, he held his AR-15, now ready for action as he looked around becoming aware of his surrounding (but nobody really looks up do they) that is when Jeff leaped from the ladder of the fire-escape as he pulled his Warrior-knife out of its sheath and landed on top of the ISD agent swiftly cutting his throat with his knife, the agent dropped the machine-gun and fell to his knees as he held his neck, blood gushed out of his neck from between his fingers like a high school water-fountain as the agent gasped for air, the ISD agent then fell over dead in a pool of his own blood. Jeff took off towards where he parked his SUV, it was parked off Clementine Avenue in a alley, Hollibase Blvd was the next main street west running parallel with Shore Street, fortunately for Jeff Hollibase Blvd was a very busy street that was full of pedestrians so Jeff ran there and hid amongst the crowd of people as he made his way to the alley where his SUV was.

President Myers was in his limo in underground parking waiting for security to get his wife, General Bankole and his daughter. Gloria, the general and his daughter were still sitting in the VIP box, they were confused in what was going on, security came and escorted them to the president's limo, a young man for the president's security came into the VIP box "we have to go" he said to Gloria as he held her arm "what's going on" Gloria asked him "there has been a shooting mam" the security officer replied "oh my god, where's my husband, is he okay" she asked the young officer as she covered her mouth with her hand in shock "he's okay mam he's in the limo but we need to leave now" the officer assured Gloria "you to sir" the officer waved over the general and his daughter to come with them. When they got back to the president's limo Gloria hugged her husband "I'm so happy nothing happened to you" she said to him and gave him a kiss on the mouth. They were all now in the limo and security closed the doors, security also had four black SUVs surround the president's limo as it headed to The Orange Gate. Leaving the outdoor entrance to the property of Hope Stadium the limo turned right onto Shore Street heading south to Bowling Dice Lane. Sitting next to her husband Gloria could feel Sterling's body trembling "are you okay honey" she asked him with concern as she caressed his semi-bloodied face with her hand discovering that the back of his suit was covered in blood "yeah just a little shaken up" Sterling replied "why, what happened" Gloria inquired "one of my security was shot and killed, he was standing behind me at the time plus a police officer was shot and killed and he was standing next to me" Sterling told her as he stared at his trembling hands "do you think it's this assassin they're looking for" Gloria asked Sterling "I don't know quite possible, I need to lay down for awhile after taken a long shower and then speak with Walt" he replied to Gloria and then kissed her on the forehead as he held her close "don't worry everything will be okay" he assured her. The limo turned right onto Bowling Dice Lane, Bowling Dice Lane was a very wide road, it has four lanes going in the same direction and four going in the opposite direction, in the center of the road were islands with concrete planters that displayed various tropical flowers and plants. "What do we do with our tickets" Dedra asked her dad "I'm sure in a situation like this anybody with a ticket will be getting a refund" David replied, Sterling who got the tickets interjected in the conversation "actually those are play-off tickets good for the whole play-offs so don't get rid of them, there's a game tomorrow at Stage Park Theater, Pearles Caimans against The Amaryllis Jets" he told Dedra. Dedra smiled and looked at her dad and then back at Sterling "thank you for the tickets President Myers" Dedra said to him "you're welcome" Sterling replied. Savannah Court branched off the north side of Bowling Dice Lane, the limo made a right turn onto Savannah Court, not too far down from Bowling Dice Lane on Savannah Court is a security-gate, standing in front of the gate were three security-guards in black army fettig holding AR-15s. The limo stopped in front of the gate, one of the security-guards went around to the driver's side window, the limo-driver rolled down the window and showed the guard his credentials "okay you can go through" the guard told the limo-driver and opened the gate. The limo entered onto what people on Janoesha Harbour call The Grounds, all the buildings on The Grounds were government, there was only one way in and out of The Grounds and that was at the gate, The Grounds were clean and neatly up kept with plush-green lawns that displayed beautiful rock-gardens.

4

THE INTERNATIONAL

After meeting with Walt Buyer on Base Laysan The Branch drove Jackson out to Bay Laurel Hedging a suburb of Brookshore in the northwest just south of Martin's Grove, The Branch has a training and field facility there. Tourist call Bay Laurel Hedging 'Bay Laurel', people that live on Janoesha Harbour call it 'The Hedging'. When Jackson gets to the training facility he was to see a Peach which he thought was an odd name for a person to possess. A grey humvee brought Jackson to The Hedging, a few miles east of Base Laysan the humvee entered onto Highway 33 that would take them into Brookshore. Jackson sat there in the humvee remembering what Walt Buyer told him "just Intel alone and try your best to minimize the risk" 'it ain't no fun without risk' Jackson thought to himself as he gave off a smirk that nobody noticed, two JHSF Officers were sitting in the back with Jackson, The Branch uses them as security for their agents. JHSF stands for Janoesian Hostage & Special Forces, they're armed with a M4 Colt Commando assault rifle and the Wilson Combat EDC X9 handgun for a sidearm, they dress in black army fettig with a black Kevlar-vest and helmet, it says JHSF in bold white letters on their vest, their job is hostage takeovers, tracking & capturing wanted fugitives and serial killers. "Who's taking care of my car when I'm gone" Jackson asked the driver of the humvee "it'll be safe in Corporal Roland's garage" the driver replied "how long do I have until I leave" Jackson asked the driver "my job is to drive you to The Hedging, I wasn't told anything else" the driver told him "didn't they tell you anything on base" the driver asked Jackson "yeah everything but that" Jackson replied. It took them just about five hours to get to The Hedging, there was a ten feet high steel electric-fence surrounding the training facility, they had to enter through a security gate, sitting in the booth beside the gate were two JHSF Officers. One of the officers walked up to the driver's side of the humvee while holding his assault rifle "how can I help you sir" he asked the driver of the humvee "I'm here on transport to handler" the driver replied and gave the JHSF Officer his government credentials "okay you can go through" the JHSF Officer told the driver as he handed him back his credentials, the gate opened up and the humvee entered onto the training grounds. "This is a big place" the driver said to Jackson "I've only been here once before and I don't remember it too well" Jackson told him "well don't worry I know how to get around here" the driver said "we're suppose to go to the Tech Building which is not that far" he told Jackson. The humvee made a left turn and then five minutes later turned right on a narrow road that was made of interlocking stone, the road snaked through a grove of shaded Elm and Mahogany-trees, when they got out of the grove of trees they entered onto plush-green meadows on both sides of the road, on a hill in the distance was a large cream colored estate-looking house with dark-brown siding "wow!" the driver said as he stared at the building through his windshield "you hit the big time here agent" he said to Jackson "you think so" Jackson replied in a coy manner. The humvee drove up the large circular driveway of the Tech Building and parked in front of its front door which were two large brown wooden doors "alright this is your stop" the driver told Jackson, Jackson grabbed his knapsack that was on the floor of the humvee and exited out the back, he stood in front of the front doors beside the humvee, the humvee's passenger side window went down "don't forget her name is Peach" the driver told him "who can forget that name" Jackson said, the driver waved goodbye to Jackson and drove off.

Peach is a forty year old lady with shoulder length black-hair and a tawny complexion, she works as a Robotics Engineer in the Tech Building and Jackson's Equipment Supplier on his mission in Cuba. She has a large office which she works out of, it is filled with mechanical gadgets, devices and robot parts. She is currently working with holographic technology, a 3D hologram that looks like a solid object, that you can walk around but not touch. She's working on combining it with telecommunications, so speaking with a relative in another country will be a whole lot more personal.

She has a contract with the International Telecommunication Union (ITU) for installment in some countries when testing is complete. Peach heard a knock at the door, she stopped what she was doing and went to see who it was, when she got to the door she opened it and saw Jackson Ames standing at the doorway "hello Agent Ames come in" she said to Jackson, Jackson followed behind her as she lead him to a group of computer-screens, she reached into the pocket of the white lab-coat she was wearing and took out a cell-phone and handed it to Jackson "here this is yours" she told him "a cell-phone" Jackson asked confused "we're going to be tracking your every movement" Peach told him "can't you just track my phone" Jackson asked her "this phone also doubles as a stun-gun, it also shoots four darts out of it" she informed him "cool but can it still make regular calls" Jackson inquired "yes but please don't overdo it, I have to pay the bill" Peach told him. Peach opened up a drawer in her desk and took out a brown-folder and put it on her desk "one more thing your cover is Matthew Perez an Installation Technician for Link/Finity an internet provider in Cuba" she informed him. Jackson picked up the folder, opened it and started reading "that's wonderful but how am I suppose to get into The Farm" he asked Peach "Link/Finity provides The Farm with internet" she told Jackson, Jackson gave her a smile. Jackson had a personal question to ask Peach so he just came right out and asked her "is Peach your real name" he asked her "it sure is, Peach McFarlen plus people say I'm a peach" Peach replied and winked at Jackson with a seductive smile on her face. Jackson could see that she is a very attractive lady "so how do you like working here" he asked her "I love it" she replied, Jackson held onto the folder as Peach escorted him to another section of her office "so I see you like dissecting robots" Jackson said to her as he looked around her office "it's my job" Peach replied as she stopped and stood in front of a closet with two wooden doors "what do you do for work" Jackson asked her curious to know "at the present time I'm your Equipment Supplier" Peach replied as she opened up the closet. Hanging in the closet were two two-piece black and grey men suits and a uniform from Link/Finity, they were covered in clear plastic "in the lining of these clothes there's a material sewn in that is bullet proof, if you get shot you'll still feel the bullet and it will leave a bruise but it won't pierce through the material" she told Jackson "cool" Jackson said "just know this only works with handguns so don't get shot by a rifle or a machine-gun because it will go through" Peach informed Jackson "thank you for the advice" Jackson said to her. "By the way who's my contact in Cuba" Jackson asked Peach "that's a good question, I was just about to get to that" she told Jackson "his name is Finch Leara, he owns a coffee shop named The Bean Depot in Bayamo" Peach replied. Peach gave Jackson a ticket for first-class flight 809 from James Starr airport in Tamerra, the departure time was 9:00 tonight, "Finch will be waiting for you at the Carlos Manuel de Cespedes Airport in Bayamo, he'll be the man holding up the sign that says Matthew Perez" she informed Jackson. Peach grabbed her keys and purse from off her desk "are you hungry" she asked Jackson "I could eat" Jackson replied not too sure where this was going "I hope you like Mexican" she said to Jackson as she opened the door and left her office, Jackson followed closing the door behind him "always a pleasure" Jackson said to himself referring to Peach's invitation to lunch. Peach took Jackson to a small Mexican restaurant that was in the basement of the Tech Building, it was about the same size as a bistro, it is named The Sombrero. They sat around a round table on a couple of stools, Jackson looked around, he was impressed "you guys have a plaza in the basement of this building, that's quite impressive" Jackson said to Peach "we have everything here even living quarters where you'll be staying until your ride comes to take you to the airport" Peach informed Jackson. Jackson shuffled his stool closer to Peach "I was hoping to stay with you until my ride came" he told her in a soft manly tone "it's nice to have hopes and dreams" she replied with a wink and a smile and then picked up one of the two menus the waitress put on the table.

A few hours went by and Jackson was now in the backseat of a Lincoln towns car being driven to James Starr Airport in Tamerra. He was wearing one of the two-piece suits Peach gave him, the grey one, he wore it with a fuscia colored shirt and matching kerchief lightly stuffed in the jacket's breast pocket on his head he wore a grey trilby. Jackson sat in the backseat reading through the folder Peach gave him, in the folder there was pictures of The Farm and outside its perimeters taking from the air, there were also surveillance pictures of a Doctor Ray Gatlain an Animal Surgeon that works at The Farm. There was no pictures of inside The Farm, the pictures of Ray Gatlain was of him at a bistro in Bayamo speaking with an unknown male person that The Branch believes is one of the coordinators at The Farm, Jackson kept looking through the folder. The Towns Car drove west on

Route 22 in Tamerra, it took them a little over four hours to get to the airport, James Starr International Airport is located at Route 22 and 53 in Tamerra, it takes up five and a half blocks ending at Route 16. The Towns Car drove up a paved ramp and stopped in front of the airports front entrance, the back door opened, Jackson grabbed a silver colored briefcase off the seat next to him and got out, he stood next to the Towns Car and straightened up his suit-jacket and made sure he still had his ticket. "Keep safe Mr. Ames" the driver of the Towns Car told him "will do" Jackson replied as he shut the car's door, the Towns Car drove off, Jackson headed into the airport to check in his briefcase and to see what entrance his flight was coming in at.

Tamerra, Janoesha Harbour

It was just after eleven at night and street-lights with their ambient glow were on throughout the Bluewinds neighborhood, Stacey had turned off the TV ready to call it a night, she went to the kitchen for a late-night snack before heading to bed, Moses had already been sleeping for the past half an hour, earlier today something went wrong with his truck's engine while he was doing some errands and he had to bring it to the mechanic's, he took the local transit home. Stacey opened up the cupboard and took out a box of chocolate-chip cookies, just then she heard the porch-light explode "what the..." she said as the noise made her jump, she held her chest trying to calm down her heart-beat as she slowly walked to the front door to see what happened, on the way to the door she saw through the obscure window beside the front door a shadowy figure, this made her scream and turn around making a run for the bedroom. Moses heard the scream and immediately sat up in bed "STACEY" he called out to her, just then he heard a loud bang like someone kicked in the front door, Moses grabbed his Glock off the night table beside the bed. Stacey ran into the bedroom and slammed the door shut behind her, she hid behind the bed "what's going on" Moses asked her, just then shots were fired from outside the bedroom that created four large holes in the bedroom door "holy shit, keep down honey" Moses told Stacey as he started shooting back. Moses got out of bed as he kept shooting at the bedroom door until there was no one firing back, he diligently went to the bedroom door and opened it, Moses slowly peeked around the corner of the open doorway. In the hallway he saw the same man he chased to Pearles a few days ago dressed all in black holding a machine-gun, (it was Jeff Acheampong) Jeff raised the machine-gun and started shooting into the bedroom, "get down" Moses told Stacey as he hid behind a dresser, Jeff took off out the front door. Moses turned into Silverback and gave chase, Silverback ran and smashed through the front door leaving a giant hole in the front of the house, when he came out to the driveway he saw three ISD agents laying dead on the ground, each agent was shot between the eyes. Silverback heard a vehicle's motor start up, he turned to see who it was, it was the same grey SUV he chased to Pearles. Silverback growled and leaped over to where the SUV was but Jeff sped off before he could get to him, the SUV headed towards Route 55, Silverback was following right behind it, he got close enough to swipe at the SUV's back bumper causing it to swerve in its lane "fucking ape" Jeff said to himself as he did his best to control the SUV from crashing. Jeff slammed his feet on the gas trying to speed away from Silverback but he couldn't the ape was too fast so when he got onto Route 55 he decided on swerving in and out of traffic, this caused Silverback to slow down because he didn't want to hurt anyone in his pursuit of Jeff Acheampong. Silverback came up with an alternative he started running on the gravel shoulder of the road just to keep up to the SUV, Jeff looked through the front passenger-side window and saw Silverback running on the gravel shoulder "TENACIOUS AREN'T YOU" Jeff called out to Silverback as he pointed his Beretta M9 at him and shot Silverback two times in the arm "that should slow you down" Jeff said to himself as he got back to focusing on the road. Shooting Silverback didn't work, Jeff didn't realize that the wounds on Silverback's arm caused by his gun took twenty seconds to heal into scabs, Silverback body-checked the SUV causing it to swerve into another lane almost getting its back-end clipped by a straight-truck.

Tamerra, Janoesha Harbour

An announcement was made over a PA System at James Starr Airport for all passengers of flight 809 to Bayamo, Cuba to enter the plane at Gate/Entrance 8. Jackson got up from where he was sitting and headed over to Gate/Entrance 8, surprising to Jackson the airport wasn't all that busy, yeah there were travelers here but he's known James Starr Airport to be shoulder to shoulder people. When Jackson got to Gate/Entrance 8 he could see that a good size line of travelers had accumulated in front of the entrance so he joined the line and stood behind a young couple on their honeymoon. A young curly haired stewardess stood beside the entrance and stamped everyone's ticket as they boarded the plane, she also welcomed them "welcome aboard Harbour Wings Air" she said as she greeted them with a smile. Jackson looked at his ticket as he boarded the plane, he saw that his seat was Seat 43, the number was posted in the center of the top section of the seat, Jackson looked for his number, he saw that his seat was a window seat and went over to it. When Jackson got to his seat he sat down and laid his briefcase on its side on a small table that was in front of his seat, an attractive middle-age lady sat down next to him in Seat 42, she was texting on her Blackberry-phone. Jackson took off his hat and rested it on his lap, he was thinking about taking a short nap before asking for something to eat. He spotted a stewardess about to walk by him "excuse me can I get some ear-plugs" he asked the young stewardess "absolutely sir" she replied as she gave him a bright smile, she reached in the jacket pocket of her uniform and took out a pare of ear-plugs still in the plastic "here you go sir" she said to Jackson as she handed him the ear-plugs. Jackson got comfortable in his seat while he put the ear-plugs in his ears, he leaned his head against his shoulder as he slouched down in his seat, Jackson reclined back the seat a bit and closed his eyes. Three and a half hours later Jackson woke up to the pilot announcing that they've entered into Cuban airspace, the pilot added that it would be another twenty minutes until they land. Jackson looked out the window and saw Cuba from a bird's-eye-view, it was as beautiful as a postcard to him. The plane began to slowly descend out of the air as it's wheels came down, it touched down on the landing-strip outside Carlos Manuel De Cespedes Airport, the plane's wings angled at 45 degrees as it came to a safe stop in front of the airport. The curly haired stewardess opened up the plane's door "make sure you gather all your belongings before exiting the plane" she told the passengers "thank you for flying Harbour Wings Air" she said to the people that were exiting the plane. Jackson grabbed his briefcase and headed out of the plane, he went to get his briefcase checked in, at the check in line they also stamped his Janoesian passport and he entered into the front lobby waiting area where he started looking for someone holding up a sign saying Matthew Perez. Inside the waiting area was busy with travelers coming and going, some meeting family, others here on business or pleasure, Jackson made his way through the crowd of people looking for Matthew Perez, he spotted a middle aged man with salt and pepper colored facial hair standing by the sliding-doors that lead outside holding up a cardboard sign that read Matthew Perez. "Hi I'm Matthew Perez" Jackson told him as he came close to the man "hi my name is Finch Leara" Finch said to Jackson as he extended his hand in friendship and chucked the sign in the garbage-can next to him with his other hand, they shook hands "nice to meet you" Jackson said. "Is that all you have, just a briefcase" Finch asked Jackson as he pointed at the briefcase he was holding "yeah that and my backpack" Jackson replied, "come on there's a cab waiting for us outside" Finch told him. They went outside and got into a lime-green cab that drove them to The Bean Depot, The Bean Depot is a coffee shop owned by Finch Leara, Finch moved to Cuba in 2018 after semi-retiring from the ACIB, a year later he bought the building which is now The Bean Depot, so I guess you can say he owns the whole building, upstairs above the coffee shop is where Finch lives and that's where Jackson will be staying while in Bayamo. The streets of Bayamo were busy with young adults going and coming from the night-clubs that were on the main strip, a lot of old cars from the fifties era filled the streets, Jackson stared through the window of the cab at the streets of Bayamo as it made it's way to The Bean Depot. The cab pulled up in front of The Bean Depot "okay here we are" Finch said to Jackson as he opened the front passenger-side door and got out, Jackson opened the back door and also got out shutting the door behind him, Finch handed the cab-driver a Purple Tanager which is a ten dollar bill in Janoesian money "gracias" he said to the driver and shut the door, the cab drove off in the opposite direction. Janoesian money is very high in Cuba, one Janoesian Rupee is worth twenty-one Pesos in Cuba, ever since the International Mining Corporation (IMC) opened up free trade in jewelry between Janoesha Harbour and Cuba the currency ratio has been at a stand-still. Finch took a bunch of keys out of his pocket and opened a green-wooden door that was next to the coffee shop, when he stepped in he flicked on a light-switch mounted on the wall to the right of him "okay lets go" he motioned to Jackson with his hand. Finch lead Jackson up a flight of stairs to a three bedroom flat with balcony "come on in and feel at home here" Finch told Jackson as he opened the door to his apartment, Jackson stepped in, inside the apartment had a Art Deco feel to Jackson. "Feel free to look around, my place is your place"

Finch told Jackson "I should probably try to get some rest" Jackson said "I got a busy day tomorrow" he added "that you have, for sure but it's not going to stop you from having a drink with me" Finch told him and then escorted Jackson up a few steps to his living room where he had a mahogany bar with a marble top, his living room floor was carpeted with white alpaca-carpet. Finch went behind his bar and took out a bottle of Mount Gay Rum, he rested the bottle on the bar and put two empty rock-glasses in front of it "have a seat" Finch told Jackson as he poured them both a drink, Jackson sat down on one of the three stools that were in front of the bar. "So how was your flight" Finch asked Jackson "okay I guess" Jackson replied "that's good, you know this Farm thing I've been on it for a few years and I must say they are good at keeping invisible" Finch told Jackson as he handed him a rock-glass. Finch raised up his glass to make a toast "may this mission lead to the downfall of The Farm" he said, they cheers! Each other and took a drink, Finch poured a little more in his glass and raised the bottle in offerance to Jackson "want some more" he asked Jackson "sure" Jackson replied as he held out his glass for more.

Alan's Landing, Janoesha Harbour

The next day in Alan Landing the President and Walt Buyer was at the veteran cemetery in Rockridge, two ISD agents were being buried after that incident at Shearwater Run. Actually what happened was a high speed chase heading north on Highway 34 resulting in an Avis rental van swerving out of control and crashing during a shootout, the shootout continued on the side of the road six miles south of Brookshore. Gunnery Sergeant Al Nambridge and First Sergeant Zane Gohobee were both killed in the shootout, all four men in the Avis rental van were killed, two were killed by gun shots the other two were killed in the crash. The funeral was done in full military honor with a twenty-one gun salute for the two soldiers that gave their lives to protect the citizens of this country. The turn out to the funeral was more than expected, over two hundred people showed up not including the service men and women that were there, it was certainly a good day for being outside weather wise, it was sunny and 32 degrees celsius with blue skies. President Myers sat down in front of the two coffins with the Janoesian flag spread out on top of them, Walt Buyer was sitting next to him with Alex Williams and Joe Anhime sitting on the other side of him "I'm getting tired of burying good men" the president said to Walt "yes I know sir, it went bad in Spirit's Cove" Walt apologized to President Myers "not to worry, they did their jobs" the president said "the main thing sir is to keep you safe" Walt told the president "and you are, right" President Myers asked Walt "yes sir we are" Walt replied. "You have it all secured at my house" the president asked Walt "yes Alex sent some JHSF Officers over there" Walt replied "how's it going over in Cuba with Jackson" the president inquired "he's getting into the routine of being an Installation Technician" Walt replied "that's good" the president said "I thought you were planning on moving Valor Grounds Cemetery to the north" Walt asked the president safely changing the subject "whatever gave you that idea" President Myers replied "a year ago there was a read up on it in the Harbour Times, it said you were thinking of moving it to north Pearles" Walt told him "yeah I remember the article, it's something that's still at the planning stage" the president said. Valor Grounds Cemetery was the cemetery they were at, Valor Grounds Cemetery was built in 1879 specifically for veterans, it's one of the biggest cemeteries on Janoesha Harbour, it's second in size to AshDove Cemetery in Amaryllis Jaiz. JHSF Officers stood guard at the front gates of Valor Grounds Cemetery as the crowd of people started to exit the cemetery, the president and Walt were still sitting in front of the two coffins "thinking of the pros and cons of this, as a con should we worry about any rebuttal from Cuba" President Myers asked Walt "the covertness of this mission will allow us to gather the required information and exit safely without notice" Walt assured the president. They both got up out of their seats and headed towards the front entrance, a couple of the president's security were following closely behind them "oh I forgot to mention, after the extraction in Namibia we sent a Body Transport to pick up two of our soldiers" Walt informed the president "were their families contacted" President Myers asked Walt "yes sir, as soon as the plane touched down in Base Laysan" Walt replied "I hate seeing the lost of young souls" the president said as he sighed in sadness at the lost of the two soldiers in Namibia "I know sir" Walt said to him. Out in front of the front gate Walt and President Myers got into a black Lincoln Limo along with the president's security, the limo made a three point turn and left the cemetery's parking lot. Body Transports are cargo-planes that pick up dead bodies of soldiers and brings them home so their families can bury them, they're used by the Janoesian Army after war as their Casualty Clean-up.

Bayamo, Cuba

At The Farm one of the security-guards for the building was about to be reprimanded for money being missing from a safe in a room next to Ray Gatlain's office, the security-guard that was about to be reprimanded name was Eduardo Nunez, he was the only guard on duty in that wing of the building at the time the money went missing, exactly four thousand pounds in British currency was missing from the safe. Two soldiers for The Farm took Eduardo out back to a plush-green field behind The Farm, they brought him to a small pond surrounded by palm-trees, Ray Gatlain was standing at the edge of the pond hold a machete in his right hand, Ray flicked away with his hand the butt of a cigarette he just finished smoking, the soldiers brought Eduardo right in front of Ray "do you know how important trust is Mr. Nunez" Ray asked Eduardo "sir there has been a mistake, Senor Gatlain I would never steal from you" Eduardo pleaded "you were the only guard on duty at the time and you know the combination to the safe plus you have keys to all the doors in that wing including my office because the company trust you, how do you explain that" Ray asked him, there was a lengthy pause, "I can't" Eduardo replied. Ray gave out a deep sigh of false constraint "okay then" Ray said and nodded to the soldiers to open Eduardo's shirt, the soldiers tore open his shirt, Ray swiped the machete across Eduardo's stomach, his stomach opened up like a zip-locked bag. Eduardo's entrails spilt out on the ground in front of him, the two soldiers pushed Eduardo's body into the alligator infested pond, Ray stood at the edge of the pond, he lit up a cigarette and watched as a group of gators tore apart the body.

Jackson was at the Link/Finity building in downtown Bayamo speaking with his boss a middle aged man that likes to be addressed as Mr. Brackett, Jackson was undercover he was going by his cover-name Matthew Perez. Matthew sat in a chair in front of Mr. Brackett's desk in his office, Mr. Brackett was sitting behind his desk "so you worked five years for Link/Finity in Kingston, Jamaica and then got transferred to Plymouth, Tobago before coming here to Bayamo, you certainly get around Mr. Perez" Mr. Brackett said to Matthew "I just go where they send me sir, sorry Mr. Brackett" Matthew replied. "Okay, do you know where you're going to be working" Mr. Brackett asked Matthew "I was hoping you would tell me" Matthew replied cleverly "you're on contract at a place named The Farm, they're looking for a personal Installation Technician, someone that they can become familiar with, you would be the only internet technician allowed on the property, sounds good" Mr. Brackett asked him "sure that's fine" Matthew replied "great, it's good to see you wearing your uniform" Mr. Brackett told him. Matthew had rented a car, an olive-green 1954 Corvette convertible, he drove it out to where The Farm was, his plan was to study the routine of the guards. Matthew parked near a secluded beach close to the west-wing of the property, he was about seventy feet away from the security-fence, he was sitting on a wooden bench that was on a neatly cut lawn, near the fence was all tall-grass leading up to where it surrounded the lawn Matthew was sitting in. Matthew was holding a pare of binoculars, he held them up to his eyes and looked through them at the guards at The Farm, he must of been there a good forty minutes before people started coming down to the beach. Matthew kept looking through his binoculars at the guards, just then a young lady sat down next to Matthew "hola" she said to him, Matthew lowered the binoculars from his eyes and turned around to see a very attractive lady sitting next to him "great day for bird-watching" she said to him "yeah not bad, have we met before" Matthew asked the lady "I've heard that line before, the answer is no we haven't met before, I just thought you sitting here alone you wouldn't mind some company" she replied "do you usually come up to men you don't know and strike up a conversation because if you do it's not a safe thing" Matthew told her, the lady smiled at Matthew as he looked into her large brown eyes "you ask a lot of questions" she told him with some giggle in her voice. Matthew gave the lady a curious-smile "what's your name mam" he asked the lady "Carmen Ayala" she replied and continued "and yours" Carmen asked Matthew "Matthew Perez" he replied "you don't come across as Cuban" Carmen said "I'm not I'm originally from Barcelona, Spain" Matthew told her "so what are you doing here in Cuba besides spying" Carmen inquired "now who's asking the questions" Matthew said cunningly to her "yes you're right I'll leave you to your business" Carmen told Matthew as she got up to leave "how will I see you again" Matthew asked her as he gave her a smile, Carmen took out of her purse she wears over her shoulder a business-card and hands it to Matthew "my number is on the back" she told Matthew and left. Matthew watched as Carmen walks away, as she walks away she turned her head and gives Matthew a smile, Matthew couldn't help staring at her and the way her hour-glass figure filled out the white-denim shorts she was wearing. Carmen Ayala is a thirty-one year old female, she was born in Santa Cruz, Cuba and grew up in Havana, she has never been married and has no kids. She served in the Cuban Army for nine years and then got hired onto G2 Cuban Intelligence where she currently works as a spy. Matthew looked at the business-card Carmen just gave him, it said that she works as a Sous Chef at the Flamingo Palms Hotel here in Bayamo, it even showed an address. Matthew put the card in his pants pocket and went back to studying the guards for an additional fifteen minutes, he sat there on the bench staring out at the water and the young couples on the beach wading in the shallow water while their little kids make sand-castles on the beach and bury their younger sibling. Matthew unwrapped an energy-bar he brought in his pack from Janoesha Harbour and began eating it, he starts work tomorrow morning at The Farm, The Branch gave him three bug-transmitters to plant when he got onto The Farm's grounds. Matthew took a Tablet out of his backpack and turned it on, an Information-Sheet came up on a Doctor Raymond Darius Gatlain, the sheet stated that Doctor Ray Gatlain was born in St. Andrews, Scotland on March 12th,1960, as a young man he studied medicine and the anatomy of several large animals at the University of Manchester for seven years, he graduated with a Masters In The Animal Anatomy, in 1995 a De Smet Exploration & Games out of Leszno, Poland hired him as their On-sight

Surgeon. "They've been at it that long" Matthew said to himself amazed at the length of time this crap has been going on as he continued to read the Information-Sheet, it said that Ray Gatlain was wanted in some countries in Europe plus the USA in the selling of animal organs on the black-market to restaurants and grocery-stores, he is also wanted in Mali for the mass-murder of a hundred and five people in a local town, the Information-Sheet showed pictures of a mass-grave with bodies dumped in it, women, children, dogs and cats it didn't matter they all were dumped in there "Wow this guy's a bad man" Matthew said as he continued reading.

Pearles, Janoesha Harbour

After the attack on Moses at his home he met up with Walt Buyer on Base Laysan who assigned Moses and Bailey Gcobani to find Jeff Acheampong and bring him in. Alex Williams sent a group of JHSF Officers to stand guard over Moses house and protect Stacey, right now Moses and Bailey was in Moses truck driving up into the Ormetha Hills "this is where you were the last time you chased him" Bailey asked Moses as he looked through the front passenger side window "yeah but I always seem to lose him around here" Moses replied. Moses and Bailey had a wanted poster picture of Jeff taken from a surveillance-camera at the airport, they had printed out forty copies and now had them on the dashboard of Moses truck. They drove on Route 62, just before getting to Route 21 Moses turned right into a Village Opening "what's going on, you hungry" Bailey asked him "this looks like a good place to put up some of these posters and ask

some questions" Moses replied "yeah you're right" Bailey
agreed as he looked around the area. There was a old
mechanic-shop and garage next to the Village Opening,
Moses parked the truck on a open graveled area next to the
Village Opening, he grabbed the posters off the dashboard
and exited the truck, Bailey came out on his side and went
around to where Moses was, Moses gave him half the stack
of posters he was holding "go check if anyone is in that
mechanic-shop then meet me back here" Moses told Bailey
"okay, it shouldn't take that long" Bailey said and left for the
mechanic-shop. Moses headed to the front door of the Village
Opening, when he got there he pushed open the door, a bell
chimed as he did so, Moses went up to the front counter
where the cashier was "hi mam I have a few wanted-posters
that I'm thinking about putting up but before that I'm going
to show you a picture and ask you if you ever seen this
person" Moses said to the young cashier "okay" the cashier
agreed, the cashier was a young lady in her twenties. Moses
showed her the picture of Jeff "oh my god, yes I have seen
him" she told Moses as she covered her mouth with her
hands in shock "okay calm down, do you remember where
you saw him" Moses inquired "right here, after we got robbed
he followed the man that robbed us out to the parking lot
and shot him in the head" she told Moses "when did this
happen" Moses asked her "a little over a week ago" she replied
"what's your name" Moses asked her "Joann, the thing is he
gave me back the cash the man stole" she replied "when he
left did he say where he was heading" Moses asked Joann "no
but I've seen him a few times in the area, he drives a grey
SUV, it's usually on Route 63 I see it, I believe he lives north

on 63, how far north I don't know" Joann replied. After speaking with Joann Moses grabbed two soft-drinks out of the store's display-fridge and a candy-bar from off a metal-rack in front of the cashier's counter, he paid for the items with a Crowned Short-tailed which is a twenty dollar bill in Janoesian money worth twenty rupees. Joann gave him his change "thank you for your time" Moses said to Joann and left the store, when he got back to his truck Bailey was waiting for him there "how did you make out at the mechanic-shop" he asked Bailey as he came up to him leaning up against his truck "it's a bust, it doesn't look like anyone's been there for the past thirty years" Bailey replied. Moses unlocked his truck with a press of a button on his key, they both got in "well I got something" Moses told Bailey and continued "I was speaking with the cashier in their, a nice lady Joann is her name, she tells me that there was a murder here a week ago, our man Jeff shot and killed a man right in the parking lot" Moses told Bailey "really!" Bailey asked "yeah right there in the parking lot she said" Moses replied as he pointed to the parking lot in front of the Village Opening "just like that, right out in the open" Bailey said "yep" Moses replied "that's cold blooded man" Bailey told Moses. Moses started up his truck and backed out of the graveled area onto Route 62 "she did say that she usually sees Jeff's SUV on Route 63 and that she believes that he might have a place north on 63" Moses informed Bailey "well that's good, I believe Pearles line ends at Route 18, so if his place is in Pearles we should find him" Bailey told Moses. Moses turned right onto Route 21 and took it to Route 63, when he got to Route 63 he made a left turn and headed north on 63. As Moses drove north on Route 63 they were heading further up into the Ormetha Hills where Route 63 looked like they had to blast through rock to build the road, there were rock formations on both sides of Route 63 with pygmy-goats and barbari-goats feeding on the bushes that grew off their cliffs "where do we start looking" Bailey asked Moses "before that I gotta get some gas" Moses replied. Bailey looked at the truck's gas-meter, it showed that it was almost empty "okay I see" Bailey said, an Oil/Mar Gas station was at the Route 20 intersection, it was coming up on Moses right "I haven't been up here in awhile" Bailey told Moses "the fresh-air is healthy up here" Moses said to him. When they got to the gas station Moses turned right into the Oil/Mar and pulled up next to a pump "looks like no one likes to work around here, everything is self-serve" Bailey remarked "aw come on Bailey it's good to be active it keeps you young" Moses told him as he got out of his truck to pump the gas "thanks for the tip, I'll be right here waiting for you" Bailey said to Moses as Moses went around the front of the truck to the pump. Bailey grabbed a soft-drink out of the plastic bag that was on the seat next to him, he twisted the cap off the bottle and started drinking. It took Moses only a few minutes to fill his gas-tank, after that he headed into the gas station's small variety-store to pay, Moses remembered to bring a picture of Jeff to show the Gas station Attendant. The Gas station Attendant rang up the cost of Moses gas "that will be forty rupees sir" the attendant told Moses, Moses handed him two Crowned Short-tailed bills "thank you" the attendant said "you're welcome, by the way can I show you a picture and maybe you can let me know if you seen the person in the picture before" Moses asked the attendant "sure" the attendant replied. Moses showed the attendant the wanted-poster of Jeff "have you seen this person before" Moses asked the attendant, the attendant took a good look at the picture "yeah I did, it looks like the guy that picks up mail here" the attendant told Moses "how sure are you" Moses asked him "about ninety-five percent" the attendant replied "there's a post office in here" Moses inquired "no a Janoesian Postal Outlet, the postman delivers the mail here and places them in those cubbyholes over there for people to pick up" the attendant replied as he pointed to a group of cubbyholes behind the counter and continued "I believe your man stays up on an escarpment at the east end of Route 19" the attendant told Moses "did you happen to notice what kind of vehicle he drove" Moses asked the attendant "it was a grey SUV I remember because the first time he pulled up out front I was waiting for a group of kids to come out of it" the attendant replied "thank you for your time" Moses told the attendant and left for the front door "what is he wanted for" the attendant asked Moses curious to know before Moses exited the store "three counts of first degree murder, so far" Moses told the attendant as he turned his head to face him. When Moses got back to his truck he saw that Bailey had drank one of the soft-drinks he had bought back at the Village Opening, Moses sat behind the steering-wheel and shut the door "you drank one of my drinks" Moses said to Bailey "sorry, I was thirsty" Bailey replied "doesn't really matter I bought one for you anyway, but you still should of waited till I offered it to you" Moses told Bailey as he started up the truck "I know, I'm truly sorry, if it makes you feel better the next round is on me" Bailey said "okay" Moses agreed in a soft voice. "So where are we headed to now" Bailey asked Moses "we have a location" Moses replied as he quickly looked at Bailey and then back at the road because they were now driving north on Route 63 "we do, where" Bailey inquired "east on Route 19 on top of an escarpment" Moses replied "it's a good thing I wore my hiking-boots" Bailey said as he stared out the passenger-side window. Moses made a right turn onto Route 19, Route 19 turned into a dirt-road the further east they drove, the road went up an incline three miles east of Route 63, at the top of the incline there's a dead end, to the right of a metal dead end sign was a narrower dirt-road leading up the top of an escarpment. Moses drove up the narrower road, the road surfaced out on top of the escarpment, the top of the escarpment was forested in Sabal-palm trees, African tulip trees and Mahogany trees along with different styled palm-bushes. The further Moses drove into the small forest him and Bailey could make out a small log and stone-cabin in the distance, in front of the cabin a grey SUV was parked "do you see that" Bailey said to Moses as he pointed to the SUV "looks like someone's home" Moses said as he slowly drove closer to the cabin "maybe we should park off to the side here, just to be on the safe side" Moses said to Bailey "sounds good to me" Bailey agreed. Moses parked the truck off the road next to some bushes "you have a side-arm with you" he asked Bailey "sure do" Bailey replied "have it ready" Moses told him, Suddenly as they were exiting the truck they heard gun shots, a couple shots shattered the truck's windshield, Moses took cover behind the truck and Bailey behind the open passenger-side door, another shot shattered the passenger-side door window and hit Bailey in the left shoulder as he drew his gun. Moses went into the pick-up of his truck and took out an AR-15 machine-gun, he then went to check on Bailey but Bailey had already made his way to the back of the truck "don't worry you'll be okay" Moses told Bailey as he tied a scarf around Bailey's shoulder to keep him from bleeding to death. "I ASSUME IT'S YOU MOSES, I KNOW ALL ABOUT YOU CAPTAIN MOSES UATOBUU" a voice called out to Moses "how does he know your name" Bailey asked Moses "I don't know" Moses replied "we have to move from here" Moses told Bailey and continued "you hide in the bushes and I'll head across the road and get his attention" Moses told Bailey "okay" Bailey agreed as he got to his feet. "YOU KNOW MY NAME WHAT'S YOURS" Moses asked the unknown voice as he ran across the road firing the AR-15 in the direction of the cabin, a few shots were returned that missed their mark "I THINK YOU KNOW BY NOW" the voice replied "YOU'RE NOT GOING TO WIN THIS JEFF THE WHOLE COUNTRY IS LOOKING FOR YOU" Moses told Jeff "SEE I KNEW YOU KNEW" Jeff said ignoring Moses pessimism. Jeff was laying on the roof of his cabin in a black ghillie-suit looking through the scope of his sniper rifle, he saw that the man that Moses came with had just laid down behind a large rock that top was covered in peet-moss, Jeff let off two shots with his Beretta M9 just so the man would stick his head up from behind the rock and that's exactly what Bailey did and a unheard shot hit him between the eyes killing him instantly. After Jeff killed Bailey he looked through his scope for Moses but couldn't find him "where are you, show yourself" Jeff said to himself as he looked through his scope. Moses had worked his way through the woods to the side of the cabin where there was an old wooden outhouse, he did his best to look and see who was in the cabin from the woods, he exited the woods and hid behind the outhouse, just then Moses saw debris coming down off the roof of the cabin but there was no wind out here, it was a still day, it stopped for awhile and then it started coming off the roof again 'I wonder if there's someone on top of the roof' Moses thought to himself. Moses saw that one of the back windows of the cabin was halfway open so he made a run for the back of the cabin, he made it there without alerting anyone, Moses climbed up through the window and into the cabin still holding his machine-gun. With his AR-15 drawn, holding it out in front of him he cleared the cabin for anyone, no one was there it was empty, just then when he was coming out of the bedroom he heard movement on the roof, Moses looked up as he pointed his machine at where the sound was coming from, it sound like a large animal was on the roof, he waited to hear it again and he did, Moses fired his weapon at the area of the roof the sound was coming from, blood leaked through the bullet holes in the roof "looks like I got something" Moses said to himself and then saw through the cabin's front window Jeff fall off the roof onto the ground. Moses quickly opened the front door and went outside to confront Jeff, Jeff saw that it was Moses and was about to pull out his Beretta M9 but not before Moses unloaded his AR-15 into him, Jeff fell over dead in his ghillie-suit.

5

CLASHING IN FURTIVENESS

Bayamo, Cuba

Nightlife in Bayamo is something to experience, Matthew left where he was staying at Finch's to get a drink at one of the bars down the street from them, he picked a place named Rancho Laberintico. Rancho Laberintico is a restaurant slash nightclub, the restaurant part of it is in the front, there's no roof over the restaurant section, the nightclub is in the back in front of a large bar. Matthew entered in the front door, he walked through the restaurant and took a seat at the bar, he looked around admiring the building's interior 'not a bad looking place' Matthew thought to himself. The bartender came up to him wearing a black t-shirt with the nightclub's name on it and black denim-shorts "welcome to Rancho Laberintico, what can I get for you" the bartender asked him "what do you have on tap" Matthew inquired "we have Cristal, Claro, Bucanero Fuerte, Cacique, what were you looking for" the bartender asked "you know what, I'll take a glass of Cristal" Matthew replied "sure, would you like a menu with that" the bartender inquired "yes please thank you" Matthew replied, the bartender went to pour Matthew's beer. Matthew sat there on his phone texting a friend he knew back on Janoesha Harbour, the bar wasn't very busy, only three people sitting at it including himself, a fourth person came and sat down next to Matthew to his right. "So we meet again" a voice said from the right of Matthew, Matthew turned to see who it was, it was the same lady he met at the beach "I just assume you'd be working right now being a Sous Chef and all for a very prestigious hotel" Matthew said to Carmen "it's my day off" Carmen told him "so do you usually drink alone on your days off" Matthew asked her "I'm single and here is on my way home, how about you, why are you here alone" Carmen asked Matthew "I'm also single and this is a nightcap for me" Matthew replied. The bartender brought Matthew his beer and a menu "here you go sir" he said to Matthew as he placed the beer and menu on the bar in front of Matthew "can I get you anything mam" the bartender asked Carmen "yes a glass of red-wine please" Carmen replied, Carmen was wearing a small black-dress with a low neckline that showed her cleavage, around her neck was dressed with aquamarine-pearls she also had matching earrings, her hair was done up in fancy African-braids, she crossed her legs elegantly as she sat on the stool. "When are you going back to Spain" Carmen asked Matthew "maybe I'm not, maybe I'm looking at real-estate here"

Matthew replied "so you're staying" Carmen inquired, Matthew let out a short chuckle "how is this relevant" Matthew asked her "so defensive, you need to relax" Carmen told Matthew "don't I look relaxed" Matthew said to Carmen knowing that he was "no but maybe I could help you with that" Carmen offered. The bartender came back with a glass of wine for Carmen, he placed the glass of wine on a coaster on the bar in front of Carmen "salute" the bartender said to her "have you decided on what to eat sir" the bartender asked Matthew "give me a few more minutes" Matthew replied "they have good food here, you should try a dish" Carmen told Matthew "sounds like you speak from experience" Matthew asked her "it pays to know your competition" Carmen replied "something I noticed, you seem well-mannered, were you educated here" Matthew asked her going into a smooth transition of subject "well I spent four years studying the Culinary Arts at the Universidad De Granma here in Bayamo" Carmen replied. They sat there at the bar drinking and talking, Matthew ordered a small basket of Seasoned-Chicken-wings which he occasionally ate as he kept in conversation with Carmen, he didn't know what to think of Carmen, 'such elegance and beauty but yet there was a sense of mystery there, something dark kept a side in a compartment for no one to see' Matthew thought to himself 'maybe Peach could help me with something like that' Matthew thought into it. Carmen admired Matthew's adventurous approach to life 'being handsome and young was also a good thing' Carmen thought as she looked into Matthew's cinnamon colored eyes "do you dance" she asked him "yeah a slow-dance sure" Matthew replied a little startled by the question "I see that there's a dance-floor in here so I thought you might like to dance" she asked him "why not, I'm game let's go" Matthew said accepting Carmen's offer as he stood up off the stool he was sitting on and took her by the hand "they also have a jukebox over there" Carmen told Matthew as she nearly spilt her drink from Matthew pulling her off the stool she was sitting on, she didn't though she managed to rest it safely on the bar before being escorted to the dance-floor by Matthew. They held each other close, dancing to a Christopher Cross song (Never Be The Same) that someone just put on the jukebox "you can dance, you're good at this" Carmen said in a giggly voice smiling up at Matthew "yeah the benefit of having a big sister" Matthew replied as he softly gave Carmen's deliciously round bottom a squeeze "oohh!" she sighed in delight "so affectionate" Carmen said to Matthew as she softly caressed his muscular chest with her hands. After a couple dances they got back to the bar where Matthew ordered himself another beer and a glass of red-wine for Carmen, after a couple drinks and some slow-dances Matthew felt more comfortable around Carmen. As the night grew older and older more people came in the club to where it became shoulder to shoulder space, Matthew decided that it was time to go "do you want to leave" he asked Carmen "and go where" she asked him "come on lets go" Matthew replied as he paid his bill and her's, he then took Carmen by the hand and lifted her off the stool into his arms. Carmen started giggling as Matthew carried her to the front entrance of the club "what are you doing, put me down" she told him. Matthew carried Carmen to an awaiting taxicab and got in, he told the taxi-driver to take them to the

Islazul Villa Bayamo, that hotel was covered under The Janoesian Government's account so he could stay there without paying but he didn't tell Carmen this. The taxi dropped them off in front of the hotel's front lobby, Matthew paid the taxi-driver and the cab left, Matthew and Carmen headed into the hotel, inside they went to the front desk where the Hotel Receptionist was "hi I have a room under Perez" Matthew told the receptionist, the receptionist checked her computer for the name Perez "here we go suite 515" she said after thirty seconds of searching on her computer, the receptionist reached into her desk drawer and took out a set of keys for suite 515 "here you go Mr. Perez, have a great time at Islazul Villa Bayamo" she said as she handed Matthew the keys. Matthew and Carmen headed to the elevator and took it up to the fifth floor. Matthew's room was a spacious one bedroom suite with a Jacuzzi in the washroom separate from the shower and a balcony that looked over Bayamo "this place is gorgeous, not to mention its worth, you must be rich or something" Carmen commented as she took a seat on the couch in the living room "no just had a little savings" Matthew replied as he went to the small bar that was in one corner of the living room "oh, well it's a nice place" she told Matthew as she crossed her sexy tanned legs and got comfortable. "Do you have anything to drink" Carmen asked Matthew, Matthew stood behind the bar looking at the various bottles of liquor on it, he picked one up that was to his liking, a bottle of Atlantico Gold Rhum, Matthew took the bottle and two empty rock-glasses over to where Carmen was sitting. "I found a bottle of Atlantico" he said to Carmen as he sat down beside her and put the two rock-glasses and the bottle of rhum on the center-piece in front of them "so you like rhum" she asked him as he poured them a glass "yeah you can say that" Matthew replied and then handed her a glass "salute" he said to her as they knocked glasses together. Carmen took a sip of her drink "mmm, very nice" she complimented Matthew on the rhum "I knew you would like it" Matthew said. Carmen had just met this man sitting next to her, she really didn't know anything about him only his name, Matthew Perez, but she was intrigued in what she saw so far in him, his mysterious and romantic personality not to mention he sound well educated "would it be impolite to say that I wouldn't mind kissing you right now" she asked Matthew as she gazed into the warm hypnosis of his eyes, Matthew smiled at her "it's not impolite at all" he told her as he to her surprise started kissing her on the lips, it then escalated into both of them touching and caressing each other. The next morning after Carmen spent the night Matthew got up early, leaving Carmen still sleeping in the bedroom, he went to the kitchen and poured himself a glass of orange-juice while he gave Peach a call on his cell-phone, the phone rang three times and Peach picked up "Peach here" she answered "hi Peach it's Matthew" Matthew said in a soft voice being careful not to wake up Carmen "how can I help you Matthew" Peach asked him "I need some background information on a Carmen Ayala" Matthew replied "sure I can do that, may I ask why" Peach inquired "I have a feeling that she might have something to do with this" Matthew told Peach "why are you whispering, is she with you right now" Peach asked with concern in her voice "don't worry we drank a bottle of rhum last night she's out cold" Matthew assured her. "Okay do you have your Tablet" Peach asked Matthew, Matthew went to get his Tablet that was in his backpack on the center-piece in the living room, he sat down on the couch and turned it on, an Information Sheet came up on the screen on a Carmen Jaidyn Ayala, there was also an inset picture of her at the top right corner of the sheet "is that her" Peach asked Matthew "yes" Matthew replied staring at the picture a little shocked, the lady in the picture was in uniform and Matthew really didn't see Carmen as that sort of person "she's G2, she was born Carmen Jaidyn Ayala on September 27th 1991 in Santa Cruz, Cuba but grew up and was educated in Havana, she was in the Cuban Army for nine years and was hired into Cuban Intelligence two years ago" Peach informed Matthew "what does the Cuban Government want with The Farm" Matthew asked not just Peach but also himself "well I just found this ad on Google, it's from a local newspaper in Bayamo, it says that the Cuban Government is watching The Farm closely in the breaking of their Land Tax Laws, it also says that there might be a corrupted faction within the Cuban Government that are voiding the sheets on The Farm's taxes, I guess this is where Carmen comes in, maybe G2 cot wind of this" Peach informed Matthew "yeah but why would a multi-million dollar organization like The Farm worry about paying land tax, there's something more to it" Matthew told Peach. There was a short pause on Peach's end "well I got you as much information as I could on her, it's up to you to find the rest, be careful" Peach told him and ended their call.

Alan's Landing, Janoesha Harbour

The next day after the shootout in the Ormetha Hills Moses met up with Walt Buyer at a bistro on the boardwalk of Esta Nova Beach in Alan's Landing. He was there to brief Walt on what happened yesterday, Walt was sitting around a table eating his breakfast and looking out at the ocean, he spotted Moses coming in "over here Captain" Walt said as he waved Moses over to his table. Moses knew that the result that came out of the pursuit for Jeff Acheampong wasn't what the Defense Minister expected but he was going to brief him anyway, now that he's a civilian 'the DM should put away that Captain bullshit' Moses thought to himself. Moses came up to Walt's table "have a seat Captain" Walt said to him, Moses sat in a chair across from Walt "you hungry, you want anything to drink" Walt asked him "just a glass of water" Moses replied. Walt stopped eating and placed his knife and fork in the empty plate, he wiped his mouth with a napkin on the table "so hopefully some good news from you today Captain" he said to Moses "yes sir some good news, we located where Jeff was staying in the Ormetha Hills, it was a cabin at Route 63 and 19, we proceeded with caution and was met with gunfire, we took position in the woods behind the truck and somehow in the heat of gunfire we split up doing our best to box him in, I hid behind an old out-stall looking for an opportunity, that's when I spotted Jeff on the roof and I could see that he didn't notice where I was so I made my way into the cabin and that's where I shot him off the roof and killed him" Moses told Walt "where was Agent Gcobani at this time" Walt asked Moses "unfortunately I found Bailey in the woods behind a large rock, the top half of his head was missing" Moses replied "well you got the bad guy and that's the important thing, even though he's dead and it would of been good if you would have brought him in alive to be questioned but he can't hurt anyone anymore and that's a good thing" Walt said "I sent Bailey's credentials to his family in Brookshore" Moses informed Walt "that's good they'll appreciate that" Walt replied. "So this thing in Cuba how bad is it" Moses asked Walt "it's pretty bad, this was all about making the Black Forest a game reserve for the illegal hunting of large animals" Walt replied "really, I thought it was backlash from two years ago" Moses said "the hit-list was probably thrown in as a bonus or to cover up what was really going on" Walt told Moses. It was all starting to make sense to Moses "the passport from Taitung, Taiwan was for Jeff, his picture was on it with a false name" Walt informed Moses "apparently that is their next hunting location" Walt told him "so this is an international thing" Moses asked Walt "I'm afraid so" Walt replied. Moses took a drink of the glass of water the waiter brought to the table "when you say their who are you referring to" Moses asked Walt "The Farm" Walt replied "right, yes I've heard of them" Moses said sitting back in his chair releasing a deep sigh of concern "don't worry Captain I've got it under control, we have an agent from the ACIB doing a soft-entry into The Farm to gather Intel" Walt assured Moses "is the president okay" Moses inquired "yes he's at a Safe-house with his family in The Hedging" Walt informed him, that information made Moses feel better. Walt had started drinking a glass of pink-grapefruit juice that he ordered with his bacon and eggs, he rested the half filled glass back on the table "you know it would have been nice to have Frank on board with this sniper thing, how's he doing" Walt asked Moses "well right now he's in Ontario, Canada at his parents place in Ajax, his dad was in the hospital for a bypass surgery so I think he's going to be there awhile" Moses told Walt "I hope everything goes well for him" Walt said. Moses moved his chair closer to the table and sat up straight "there's something I've been meaning to ask you, you understand I'm no longer with the military, my last duty was four years ago" Moses asked Walt "I'm aware of that and we thank you for your additional help" Walt replied "so why do you address me as Captain" Moses asked "you earned that title but if you rather me call you by your first name that could be arranged" Walt replied "I would" Moses told him "so I heard you're tying the knot soon" Walt asked Moses "yes Stacey Lane, she's a crime-journalist for TJNX News in Tamerra" Moses replied, thinking about Stacey always brought a smile to his face "well if I don't see you before the wedding congratulations" Walt told him as he raised his glass of grapefruit juice and took a drink. Moses looked out at the calming waves of the ocean and the beach "it's nice out here, not too many people on the beach this morning" Moses said to Walt "yes very nice" Walt agreed as he watched as a young attractive lady wearing a thong bikini on the boardwalk try to get away from her boyfriend slapping her pretty round bottom, the lady giggled as she felt her boyfriend's slaps "it's still early yet, it will pick up" Walt told Moses as he put on his sunglasses "come on lets go for a walk" he told Moses as he got up from around the table.

Bayamo, Cuba

After Carmen left in a taxi Matthew called for her Matthew changed into his Link/Finity uniform and called himself a taxi to bring him to The Farm. He grabbed his technician's kit off the kitchen counter and put three bug-transmitters in the kit, he was planning on planting them in different sections of The Farm. The taxi driver called Matthew to let him know that he was out front, Matthew headed out, locking the door behind him, he took the elevator down to the main floor and headed outside to where his taxi was waiting. It didn't take the taxi driver that long to get to the front gate of The farm, Matthew got out of the taxi and the taxi made a three point turn and left in the opposite direction. At the front gate there were two security-guards sitting in a booth holding machine-guns, one guard came out to see what Matthew wanted "how can I help you sir" he asked Matthew with a serious look on his face, Matthew showed him his Link/Finity ID "I'm the Installation Technician you requested for the internet" Matthew replied. The guard radioed into The Farm on his walkie-talkie he had hooked onto a belt around his waist, he asked Ray Gatlain about someone from Link/Finity coming here, Ray told him it was okay that he was aware of it. The guard opened the gate for Matthew "they're waiting for you at the main house" the guard told Matthew, Matthew headed up to The Farm's main house, when he got to its large front door he rang the doorbell that was on a metal panel mounted on the wall to the left of the door, thirty seconds later a young lady wearing a maid's uniform opened the door "come in Senor Gatlain is waiting for you" she told Matthew, Matthew stepped into the indoor lobby of the main house "please take off your shoes and follow me" she instructed Matthew, Matthew took off his sneakers and followed her, she escorted him to the study-room where Ray Gatlain was sitting behind his desk enjoy a rock-glass filled with Chivas Regal scotch whiskey and two ice cubes, he was watching CNN News on the flat-screen TV mounted on the wall to the right of his desk. "Senor Gatlain Mr. Perez is here" the maid informed Ray, Ray turned off the TV with the remote that was on his desk, he turned his head to see Matthew standing in front of his desk "oh hi Mr. Perez welcome to The Farm" Ray greeted him "please call me Matthew" Matthew told Ray. Ray took a drink of his glass "have a seat Matthew" Ray offered Matthew a chair, Matthew took a seat "so your here to fix our internet" Ray asked him "well not only fix it but keep it up and running and make it faster" Matthew replied "how are you going to do that" Ray inquired "through installing fiber-optic cables and without pinching the cable to slow down the speed" Matthew explained to him "it sounds like you know what you're doing" Ray said to Matthew. Matthew smiled at Ray's compliment "yes senor I was trained well" Matthew told Ray "so when are you planning on starting" Ray asked Matthew "I was hoping to start right away" Matthew replied "why don't you get settled in first, since you're going to be here for a week, the maid has prepared a room upstairs for you" Ray told Matthew "thank you" Matthew said to Ray. Ray took another drink of his glass of scotch whiskey "where are you from Matthew" Ray asked Matthew "Spain" Matthew replied "really! I've been to Spain, where about are you from there" Ray asked him "Barcelona" Matthew replied "okay the big city" Ray said "what were you doing in Spain senor if you don't mind me asking" Matthew asked Ray, there was a short pause and Ray gave Matthew a cautious look "well I did some work in the town of Cercedilla near Madrid" Ray replied. The maid came back "are you okay Senor Gatlain" she asked Ray "Mirana can you escort Matthew to his room" Ray instructed the maid "si senor" Mirana complied, Matthew went with Mirana to his room. Matthew followed Mirana up a spiraling bannister to a hallway, she escorted Matthew down the hallway to the second door on the right, she opened up the door and stepped to the side to let Matthew in "this is where you will be staying for the week you are here" she informed Matthew. Matthew stood inside the door and looked around the room, it was a 14ft by 10ft bedroom with a large bay-window and hardwood floor, the window looked out over the backyard of the house. "If you need any fresh towels or anything just ring that bell that's on the night table" Mirana told Matthew as she pointed to the night table "thank you" Matthew told her as he sat on the bed and put his knapsack and work-kit on the floor "lunch is at 1:30 downstairs in the dining room" she informed Matthew as she left the room closing the door behind her. Matthew sat on the bed looking through the window at the beautiful sunny day outside, he was planning on planting a bug-transmitter in the room. He started putting stuff that was in his knapsack in one of the night tables, while he put stuff in the night table he very slick and covertly stuck a bug-transmitter on the inside roof of the night table, concerned that there might be a hidden camera in here 'one down two to go' Matthew thought to himself. Next to the bed on the right was a short 4ft tall wooden bookshelf, there was three complete series of books on it, one was Nikki's and Cracker Jack's Great Cuban Adventure and the other was Sugar, Sex and Slaughter by Robert Deis, the third one was Don Pendleton's Stony Man Doctrine, that one got Matthew's attention, he remembered reading some of those books back in junior high, he loved the character Mack Bolan back then but once again with concerns about someone watching he picked up one of the Sugar, Sex and Slaughter books. After an hour of being propped up against a pillow reading Matthew put down the book and got off the bed, he decided on going for a walk around the grounds, he sat on the edge of the bed and put on a brown-leather pair of sandals he had in his knapsack along with a black silk button up short sleeve shirt to go with his tan colored pants that was made of hemp material. Matthew headed out the room and into the hallway, he went back down the spiral staircase to the ground floor, Mirana met him when he walked by the entrance to the kitchen looking for a door leading to the backyard "is everything okay Mr. Perez" she asked Matthew "I'm alright just feel for some air, is there a door leading out back" he asked Mirana "yes it's right in the kitchen here" she replied as she directed him to a set of crystal sliding-doors with the picture of a flamingo engraved on them in the kitchen. Matthew slid open the door to let the outdoor air in, the door led out to a large backyard with a neatly cut lawn and fruit-trees like orange, mango and pistachio, at the far right section of the backyard was densely populated with palm-bushes and four or five sabal-palm trees and what looked to be a pond in the mids of the foliage. Matthew stepped out into the backyard and Mirana closed the door behind him, Matthew just needed some air to think about where to plant the other two bug-transmitters, he went for a slow stroll towards the pond 'what a perfect place to think, I bet they have pretty fishes in there' Matthew thought to himself. Matthew had his cell-phone on him, he took it out of his pants pocket and texted Finch a message saying that he was at The Farm, he knew Finch knew what to do with it. He couldn't call Peach because they were probably tracing his cell-phone calls but through Peach knowing where he is she can most likely tap into his phone's frequency, Matthew put the phone back in his pocket. The warm Caribbean-air on his face made him feel healthy as he walked 'maybe I'll meet up with Carmen later and find out what she knows about The Farm' Matthew thought to himself, more like pump her for information seeing that she can't be fully trusted. Matthew is disappointed that Carmen turned out to be a G2 Agent 'but she still could be helpful' he thought to himself, he now could see the clear-blue water of the pond just behind the palm-bushes and the trunks of two Sabal-palm trees. The closer he got to the pond he could see that there were large square stones around its perimeter, Matthew was thinking about going in for a dip before he seen an eleven feet long alligator crawl out of the pond "just like Pearles I guess" he said with farce in his tone. Matthew decided that the pond wasn't the best place to think so he sat on a old 1920's style cast-iron park-bench that was on the lawn just forty feet away from the pond, he sat there just taken in the mid-day sun 'I suppose the study would be a good place to plant one of the bugs but not just yet, not until I find out the doctor's daily routine' Matthew thought to himself. Matthew sat on the bench awhile, up until Mirana called out to him informing him that lunch was ready. On the dining room table they had different types of sandwiches, Pan con timbas, Medianoches, Fritas and Chimichurri Burgers, to drink they had Papaya Smoothies, Soursop Juice, Frozen Kappa Colada Cocktails and a selection of bottled soft-drinks. Matthew sat in a vacant chair around the dining room table, around the table with Matthew were three men, two of them looked to be European, maybe from eastern Europe, the third guy looked to be from northern Africa 'maybe Libya' Matthew thought to himself, he just assumed that they were hunters lodging here in the off season. Matthew grabbed a Chimichurri Burger and rested it in the empty plate that was in front of him, he then took a Frita and started eating it "looks like someone is hungry" one of the European men said to Matthew, Matthew grabbed a bottled soft-drink twisted off its cap and started drinking "yeah it just looks so good" Matthew replied as he rested the half filled bottle on the table. Matthew noticed that Doctor Gatlain wasn't at the table, he remembered seeing him just before he got to the table, he went down into the basement with four men carrying a wooden chest and he hasn't come back up "so what do you do" the man from northern Africa asked Matthew "I'm an Installation Technician for Link/Finity" Matthew replied "Link/Finity" the man inquired "yeah it's an internet provider on the island" Matthew explained to him. "That's good your here to provide us with satellite-cable so we can watch the Playboy Channel" the man from northern Africa asked Matthew in a joking and patronizing way, before Matthew could reply one of the men from Europe interjected "now Harmon lets not be rude to the staff" he said "that's okay, if Senor Gatlain wants satellite-cable then that's what I'll give him" Matthew told Harmon as he bit into his burger and Harmon started drinking a glass of Soursop juice. The men from Europe started eating, one of them was eating a Pan con timba and the other was eating a Medianoche, they were both drinking Papaya Smoothies. Matthew sat there speaking with the men for the better part of an hour, he found out that they were actually hunters (so his assumption was right) that they were there waiting to be sent out on an expedition in the Blue Mountains of Jamaica. He also found out that Harmon is from Algeria and the two European men are Swedish, other than that they didn't give him any other information, they were very furtive around the table. When everyone was finish eating Mirana came back into the dining room "I going to leave the food on the table so if you need a snack later when you're in your rooms you can come down and take something, I'm only leaving the food here for two hours after that I clear the table and get ready for supper" she informed them. "Thank you for a great lunch" Matthew said to Mirana as he got up from around the table, she gave him a thank you-smile. Matthew went upstairs to his room, when he got there he sat on the bed and watched Forensic Files on the TV that was in the room, the TV was sitting on a dresser in front of the foot of the bed. Matthew wasn't really watching the TV he was pretending to, he was really thinking about the chest those men were carrying down the basement with Doctor Gatlain 'it looked big enough to hold a body or maybe there's money in it, he probably has a safe in the basement' Matthew thought to himself. After near to an hour of pretending to watch TV Matthew went down to the dining room to grab a Frita and a soft-drink, he took a bug-transmitter with him, on his way to the dining room he went into the kitchen, no one was there so he pretended to look for something just in case someone was watching or listening, he covertly planted the bug under the edge of the Island countertop that protruded out a inch and a half from its base. Matthew then went into the dining room and grabbed a Frita and a soft-drink, he headed back upstairs to his room to eat the Frita and his soft-drink.

AFTER THE RUCKUS

Spirit's Cove, Janoesha Harbour

Moses took Stacey to Guillman's Bay Township a suburb of Spirit's Cove in the west before you get to Alan's Landing. Guillman's Bay Township is one of Janoesha Harbour's many tourist-traps, there are houses there made of raw-stone and clay with dry-grass mixed in it, they were built by the natives hundreds of years ago, a hamlet where the natives lived, there was a small church with a schoolhouse beside it. The Federal Historical Committee on Janoesha Harbour preserved the buildings and turned the grounds into a historical village with a large stone plaque in the center of the village explaining its history. The main road in the township is Route 7, it runs from north to south straight down the middle of the township. At the south end of Route

7 is a park with a white-gazebo and south of that are large rocks that lead to the ocean, lots of kids search for starfish and oysters on the rocks. The park isn't too big but a fare size, it has neatly cut plush-green grass with pink and white Lilac-trees, surrounding most of the park were various tropical flowers and palm-bushes. Moses and Stacey were sitting on a large white blanket Moses spread down for them "it's so beautiful here" Stacey said to Moses as she laid on her back, wearing her sunglasses taken in the sun's rays "I thought you'd like it here" Moses replied as he took a Blue Toucan out of the cooler they brought with them. Stacey sat up and took an apple out of the cooler, she used a napkin she had in her purse to wipe the moister off of it "getting hungry honey" Moses asked her after taking a drink of his beer "a little I guess" Stacey replied just before taking a bite out of her apple "so I guess there's no more threat now that Jeff has been eliminated" She asked Moses "I believe Jeff is just a piece of the problem" Moses replied "they might need your help with other things pertaining to this" Stacey asked Moses in a concerned tone "I've already told you I'm not going back to the military, I'm getting married soon" he assured her, they held each other and kissed. "You're looking forward to becoming a family-man" Stacey asked Moses looking up into his eyes while they held each other "sure, growing old with a beer-belly and a wife and three kids and a urge to raid the fridge" Moses jokingly replied. Stacey gave him a light-punch on the shoulder "stop! It's not going to be like that" she told Moses, Moses held his shoulder "wow! you pack quite a punch" he told her "I know honey I'm happy to be getting married" Moses assured her and then gave her a kiss.

"Is the president okay" Stacey asked Moses "yeah, him and his family is at a safe-house" Moses replied "at lease now that Jeff is dead he can take his family home" Stacey said "not quite, do to safety precautions it's protocol for the president in these situations to spend six months in the safe-house" Moses told Stacey "so they can't go home for six months, that's horrible" Stacey said to Moses "it's not too bad, the safe-house is a two bedroom bungalow a lot smaller than his house but still comfortable" Moses told her. Moses finished off the beer and put the empty bottle next to the cooler, he sat on the blanket and stretched out his legs in front of him, he still felt tense from chasing Jeff up in the Ormetha Hills "are you okay honey" Stacey asked him "yeah I'm just trying to get comfortable" Moses replied "are you hurt" Stacey asked concerned "no just still feeling tense from chasing Jeff" Moses replied. Moses laid there on his right side, with his left hand he took out of his pants pocket two tickets to see Danforth Haynes at Stage Park Theater, Danforth Haynes in a fifty-three year old Blues singer and songwriter that plays the piano and harmonica, he's originally from Beryl Rado, Janoesha Harbour, he rose to fame back in 1989 with his hit song The Caiman Romp. Moses knew that Stacey was a big fan of the Blues from the Muddy Water and Charlie Parker CD collection she has at home, he showed her the tickets "what's this" she asked him as she took them and looked at them "two tickets to see Danforth Haynes" Moses replied "wow! How did you know I liked him" Stacey said as she looked at the tickets with a big smile on her face "I have my ways" Moses replied "Stage Park Theater I've never been there but I heard it's really nice" Stacey said as she turned and looked at Moses "so we'll go then" Moses told her with a smile "thank you" she said to him as they hugged each other and then started kissing.

Bayamo, Cuba

After taking a shower Matthew decided on going out to the backyard for a little air, there was little over a hour left until supper. Matthew opened the sliding-door to the backyard and stepped outside, the warm early evening breeze felt great to him. He went for a stroll up to where the pond is, he felt okay being next to the pond now that he's aware that there's gators in it. When Matthew got close to the pond he went and stood at its rocky perimeter, he stood there staring into its thick-blue water taken in the evening breeze and thinking about stuff, he was really thinking about Janoesha Harbour, Tamerra to be exacted, he was getting a little homesick but he knows he has a job to do. Matthew liked the reflection the palm-leaves made on the water, he stood there staring at the water 'I guess all the gators are sleeping' he thought to himself, just then the dead body of a lady floated up to the surface of the pond, there was a shoe-lace wrapped tight around her neck, the lace's aglets were two long steel needles shoved deep into her eyeballs, the lady was wearing a cheshire-pink dress. Matthew took a closer look at the body, it was Carmen "holy shit!" he said under his breath, just then an alligator bit into the body's torso and pulled it down into the water. This made Matthew feel sick and he threw up in the pond, he then went over to the bench and sat down holden his stomach while dry-heaving 'why' he thought to himself 'who would do something like this' he kept thinking, but he knew the answer to that after reading Doctor Gatlain's file. 'She was probably in the chest they carried downstairs' he thought to himself. Matthew slowly got back his stature, he stood up and made his way back inside, when he got inside he went upstairs to his room and laid down on the bed, he laid there on his back looking up at the ceiling thinking about Carmen and planting the third bug-transmitter, he knows there's a washroom on the main floor but he doesn't know where it is, and Matthew was planning on planting the final bug-transmitter in Doctor Gatlain's office (ballsy I must say). He got the last bug out of his backpack and discreetly slipped it into his pants pocket, Matthew laid back down and waited until Mirana called out for supper. 'They didn't have to do Carmen like that' Matthew thought as he laid on the bed 'this last bug will be for her' Matthew thought to himself as he did his best to control his emotions and not break down crying.

Mirana finished dressing the dining room table for supper, the table was dressed with a selection of Cuban dishes served buffet-style for everyone to help themselves, there was Spanish kenken and Rice, Cuban-Style Picadillos, Cuban Mojo Marinated Pork, Fricase de Pollo and Ropa Vieja, for desert there was Pastelitos de Guayadas, Dulce de Leche Cortada, Cuban Churros and Coquitos, there was also a choice of various bottled soft-drinks. Mirana called out to everyone letting them know supper was ready.

Matthew heard Mirana and got up an left his room, he headed downstairs to the dining room, on the way to the dining room he saw Mirana standing in the hallway leading to the kitchen "excuse me can you tell me where the washroom is down here" he asked her "yeah you go the opposite way down this hallway, it will take you around to where it ends and it's the door to your left" Mirana replied "thank you" Matthew said to her and left in the opposite direction. Matthew made his way to the washroom, when he got there he noticed the first room to the right before he got to the washroom was Doctor Gatlain's office, he knew that from the name on the door 'Doctor Raymond Gatlain' the name read mounted on the door. Matthew stood in front of the door looking down the hallway and taken a second to think 'there's probably cameras in this hallway and even though this door is slightly ajar and it looks like no one's inside there's probably cameras inside there to' he thought to himself. Matthew stooped down and pretended to tighten the straps of his sandals, as he did so he discreetly took the bug out of his pants pocket and with a little slight-of-hand he planted the bug under the bottom of the door to Doctor Gatlain's office, the bug-transmitter was planted where the door didn't quite touch the floor. After he planted the bug Matthew went back to the charade of tightening the straps of his sandals, he stopped, stood up straight as he straightened up his shirt and headed to the washroom.

Doctor Gatlain was sitting at the head of the dining room table, sitting around the table with him were four hunters that were staying at the house on their off season. Doctor Gatlain noticed that Matthew wasn't at the table "where's our technician" he asked Mirana referring to Matthew "he went to the washroom Senor, he should be coming soon" she replied "well if he doesn't he's missing a good spread" Ray said to Mirana, Mirana took it as a compliment "thank you Senor Gatlain" she said to him as she stood to the left of him in a meek stance with her head looking down submissively and a modest smile on her face. Ray poured himself a rock-glass of Chivas Regal scotch whiskey, just then Matthew walked into the dining room "there you are, we thought you might of gotten lost" Ray said to Matthew "must of drank too many liquids, had to use the washroom" Matthew informed him as he took a seat around the table, Mirana excused herself from the dining room "Senor if you need me I'll be upstairs folding clothes" she informed Ray before she left. Matthew helped himself to some food "so how do you like the place Matthew" Ray ask Matthew as Matthew grabbed a bottled soft-drink "it's okay I guess" Matthew replied "you did take a look around I hope, I mean it's quite a beautifully built house" Ray inquired "well I did check out the pond in the backyard earlier today" Matthew replied, Ray did a quick pause, given Matthew a cold stare while taking a drink of his scotch whiskey "beautiful isn't it, back there" he said to Matthew. Matthew sat there eating his food and smiling on the inside, knowing very well that he had all his angles covered, now all he has to do is play his role to the bitter end and get out safely.

THE END

Printed in the United States
by Baker & Taylor Publisher Services